THE HEARTWOOD CHEF

A HEARTWOOD SISTERS NOVEL (CARTER'S COVE BOOK 5)

ELANA JOHNSON

ISBN-13: 978-1-953506-28-3

1

Gwen Heartwood paused just inside the doorway, the temperature in the kitchen almost hotter than outside. But that wasn't why she'd stopped out of sight. No, that was so she could take a long, deep breath of the scented air.

It always smelled a little bit like Teagan's cologne in the morning, before everyone else arrived and before the true cooking began. He beat her to work almost everyday, and she'd given up trying to be the first one in the kitchens at The Heartwood Inn. As far as anyone else knew, she was first and he second, as they all arrived after the two of them anyway.

Gwent tried to push the maddening man out of her mind as she rounded the corner and went into her office. He didn't have one of those, and until a few months ago, they'd actually shared.

Shared a lot of things, actually.

A pang of sadness hit her, but she straightened her shoulders and pushed it away. *Not today*, she told herself. September had arrived, and it was time to get over Teagan Hatch. The end. Nothing more to it.

And for the first time in many weeks, Gwen actually thought she could do it. Her phone brightened with a text, but she ignored it. She knew who it would be from, and she wasn't in the mood to converse with her sister quite yet.

She sighed as she scooped her hair up into a ponytail. She had a lot of pale blonde hair, but it was very fine, and her heart swooped as she realized how tiny of a ponytail she made. Celeste had gorgeous hair, but she hated how she had to baby it so much. Gwen had learned over the years that everyone hated their hair. Women with curly hair wanted it straight, and those with straight hair wanted it to curl.

So she wished she had more hair than she did, while one of her best friends hated how thick her hair was—especially in the summer.

Gwen looped the ponytail up again and secured it a second time to keep her hair out of the way for the day. She donned her white chef's jacket, though she really just wanted to wear her T-shirt with a cartoon crab on the front.

But Teagan would be in his jacket, and by the way the

air was now scented with onions and bacon, he'd already started the frittatas for their brunch buffet that morning. The hotel hosted dozens of conferences each year, and this breakfast buffet was for a small group of technology influencers staying at the hotel until Sunday.

She loved coming to work in the restaurant, but she sat down at her desk and pulled the schedule in front of her, so she'd look busy if someone came in. No one would. Everyone in the main kitchen knew exactly what time to arrive and exactly what to do once they did.

The outside door opened with its loud squeal, signaling the arrival of someone else. Gwen didn't need to guess who it was. Gage Sanders had taken over as the head pastry chef about six weeks ago, and he almost beat Gwen to work some days.

He claimed it was because he didn't sleep well, and Gwen was an early-riser too. Her sister, Sheryl, who was Gage's girlfriend, was not. Neither was Celeste, and Gwen wished she could stay home until ten o'clock in the morning.

Out of all the sisters, only Olympia worked more than Gwen did, and honestly, she was tired.

Only thirty years old, and tired already. Alone, and tired.

The adjectives were only getting more negative, and Gwen derailed her train of thought before she started spiraling again.

Besides, she had a new prospect for a boyfriend. Celeste had hosted a Love to Forty tennis event for singles at the inn a few weeks ago, and Gwen had gone. She'd met a few men there, and she'd been going out with anyone who asked. One man had asked a few times, and Gwen didn't entirely hate hanging out with Daniel Jenkins.

"He's certainly not Teagan," she muttered, immediately hating the words and wishing with everything in her that they weren't true.

Unable to distract herself with mindless administrative tasks, she got up and went into the kitchen. Gage worked at his station, his hands sure and his movements precise though he had no formal culinary training.

Gwen had gone to culinary school, but she could appreciate raw talent when she saw it. And Gage had it, as even the guests had started to notice the different bakery items his mind had come up with.

Gwen had worried about her sister's departure from the inn, but she now envied Alissa. Gwen didn't want to leave the family business. Not really. But she certainly needed a break. A vacation from her own life.

But she couldn't have one today. No, today, she was on the room service orders, and she stepped over to the stainless steel counter where she'd put together the items the delivery waitresses needed.

Scrambling eggs and pouring juice was easy work, and she loved the tiny little salt and pepper shakers, miniature bottles of ketchup, and the smell of bacon and sausage that came from her station.

Once she completed those orders, she'd attend a meeting with Teagan, as it was Friday, and he had a house special for Redfin every weekend. As the executive chef, it was his job to make sure everyone knew about the items from his sous chefs to the waitresses.

"Eggs benedict," he called, and no one responded.

Gwen glanced around the kitchen, which had moved into its hot breakfast service for the bakery. Redfin, their on-site flagship restaurant, was only open for lunch and dinner, and Gage stocked all the baked goods in the bakery. But they also offered a short selection of hot items that Teagan made in between his other work, whether that be the catering or the meal prep for lunch and dinner.

Gwen stepped around her prep station and watched as Lilly, the petite brunette who'd put in the eggs benedict order stood by the window, obviously trying to catch Teagan's eye. She was Gwen's opposite in every way, from the color of her hair to the curves she sported to how easily she could flirt with a man and walk away with a date.

Except for Teagan, obviously, as the man barely glanced at her. "We'll get it done, Lilly," he said.

She giggled, and Gwen rolled her eyes. "Do you need help?" she asked, trying not to focus on Teagan's gorgeous hair. The color of wet sand, his hair hung around his face, and he sometimes smoothed it back into a manbun that left every female who saw him swooning.

Gwen included, unfortunately.

"I'm not sure where Gordon went," Teagan said without looking at her. His voice took on a dead quality, almost a monotone. The same *I'm-bored* voice he'd been using with her in the kitchen since they'd broken up.

Gwen's pulse skipped over itself. "He went out on the floor," she said, nodding out the service window.

"Why would he do that?" Teagan's hands flew as he garnished a plate of pancakes with powdered sugar and set them in the window. Lilly didn't move to take the order out, instead still smiling at Teagan. "He's on the egg station this morning."

"I can do it," Gwen said. "And Lilly, you might as well give up. Teagan doesn't date."

Lilly's mouth rounded, she grabbed the plate of pancakes, and walked off. Satisfied, Gwen turned to the egg station. No, she hadn't made a poached egg for a while, but she certainly knew how. Her expensive New York City culinary education had taught her that much.

"I date," Teagan barked.

"You do?" Gwen laughed. "Since when?"

"You don't know what I do after I leave here," he said.

"Yes, I do," Gwen said. "Same as me. You drag yourself home after cooking for six straight hours and you collapse onto a couch somewhere, eating whatever you can find easily." She met his sea green eyes, almost daring him to contradict her. Or maybe she just wanted to swim around in those pretty eyes. She wasn't sure which.

"Then you come back and do it all again, only this time for eight hours." She cocked her hip and dared him to contradict her.

He didn't, which meant she'd spoken true.

"You've been going out a lot lately," he said coolly.

Gwen blinked, because she wasn't sure what to do with what he'd said. He'd noticed? "Who have you been out with lately?" she asked, treading on very dangerous ground now. The last woman Teagan had been out with had earned herself a new stalker—at least for a few hours while Gwen searched and read everything the woman had ever posted on social media.

That hadn't ended well. In fact, Gwen distinctly remembered the stomachache she'd had after eating an entire carton of double chocolate fudge ice cream during the search.

She didn't mean her question to be a challenge, but Teagan's chin lifted, his way of saying, *Challenge accepted.*

Everything between the two of them was a challenge, and Gwen was tired of that too.

He didn't answer the question, instead saying, "Eggs benedict," again.

"Yes, chef," she recited back to him, tearing her gaze from his. She hadn't asked him who he'd dated since her, but she already knew that answer: No one. In fact, in the five years Gwen had known the dark, mysterious, handsome Teagan Hatch, he'd only been out with the woman Gwen had looked up. Just her.

And then Gwen.

No one else.

As she poached the eggs, she couldn't help remembering those few months. They'd been amazing, filled with wonder and excitement as she learned more about the man who could put out a plate of delicious food better than anyone she'd ever met. She'd seen his soft side, and his funny side, and his adventurous side, and she'd liked them all.

Too bad he'd broken up with her out of the blue, with absolutely no explanation at all. And the man was a vault when he wanted to be. He could shut down faster than a convenience store at closing time, and Gwen hadn't been able to crack his stoic exterior since.

Her only comfort was that no one else had either—not even the giggly, voluptuous Lilly. In her chef's jacket, Gwen looked more like a man than a woman, which had become a reason to keep her hair as long as possible. Oh, and she wore oversized earrings everyday too. That helped her feel and look more feminine.

"Eggs benedict," she said, placing the dish in the window, her body getting dangerously close to Teagan's.

He cut a look at her out of the corner of his eye, and Gwen pulled in a breath and held it. Time slowed, and when it came roaring back to full speed, she stumbled.

"Whoa," she said, her head spinning. She grabbed onto Teagan's arm, and unfortunately, he'd reached for her plate of eggs in the window.

The next thing she knew, they were both on the floor, covered in hollandaise sauce and runny egg yolks.

2

Teagan Hatch had never fallen so fast—unless the last time he'd allowed himself to get tangled up with Gwen Heartwood counted. He'd definitely fallen fast then—right in love with her.

Working with her every day since their relationship had ended had been torture, but he couldn't give up the head chef job at the most prestigious inn within three hundred miles. And he wouldn't go back to Whistlestop Shores.

Oh, no, he would not.

"I'm so sorry," Gwen said, pure shock in her voice. Teagan wiped the hot sauce off his arm and looked at her. A beautiful flush stained her neck and face, turning her from a pale goddess into an embarrassed woman in less than a moment.

He wanted to laugh. He wanted to kiss her. He wanted

to assure her everything was fine, and they could go to lunch later, and maybe he'd kiss her after their staff meeting.

He did none of those things. Instead, he swallowed the feelings that had been needling him with greater strength lately and said, "It's okay, Gwenny. Let me—" He froze, realizing too late that he'd used her nickname.

Their eyes met, and he could see everything in her mind in that moment. He'd known she wasn't over him, just as he'd known he wasn't over her. He hadn't even tried to get over her—because he'd been the one to end things between them.

And when she'd asked why...yeah, Teagan couldn't tell her.

He cleared his throat and ducked his head just as Gordon came back into the kitchen. "What's going on? What happened?" His presence broke the tension between Gwen and Teagan, and he let the other chef help him to his feet. Together, they got Gwen standing too, and she moved over to the sink to clean up.

With Gordon's help, Teagan got his station cleaned up and a fresh plate of eggs benedict out to the customer. "I'll be back in a minute," he said, untying his apron and tossing it on the table before he strode out of the kitchen.

He went down the hall and outside, where the wide, Atlantic Ocean spread before him. He drew in a breath, counting all the way to ten to do it. And he could finally breathe. "What was that?" he asked himself.

He had a reason for breaking up with Gwen. He just hadn't wanted to tell her. Because if he told her, then he'd be telling her what he didn't want her to know.

He sighed, thinking of the person who'd caused him to get too deep inside his mind. He wasn't ashamed of his daughter—he just hadn't told anyone on Carter's Cove about her. And since Gwen was only ten years older than his daughter, Teagan worried about what her reaction would be.

Those thoughts had spiraled and coiled until he couldn't bear the thought of telling Gwen about Abby. Of course, the months since had been completely unbearable too, so he wasn't sure what he'd saved.

His pride.

He dropped his head and studied the sand strewn across the sidewalk here. His watch buzzed, but he ignored it. Yes, he'd be late for staff meeting, but everyone could wait. Alexa worked the lunch shift, and as soon as the meeting ended, Teagan could go.

He worked two shifts at the inn, and he liked having the majority of the day to do what he wanted. Sometimes he laid on the beach, and sometimes he took a nap, and sometimes he went next door and made a week's worth of meals for Sheila, the widow he counted as his only outside-of-work friend.

When he finally felt centered enough, he went back inside, ready to talk about the Friday night specials he'd concocted for Redfin.

He'd only taken two steps when he heard Gwen's giggle. His heartbeat jumped, because he'd been dreaming of that giggle for months. He hadn't even tried to go out with someone new, because he knew one thing about every woman he met: They weren't Gwen Heartwood.

And the real Gwen Heartwood was currently hugging another man. Daniel Jenkins. He was nowhere near good enough for Gwen, and Teagan couldn't believe she saw anything in the man at all. A piece of driftwood had more personality, for crying out loud.

And yet, she smiled at him and waved as he walked down the hall. Teagan glared at the man as he walked away, but Daniel was so oblivious, he just smiled the whole way down the hall.

Teagan passed him, and his eyes met Gwen's. "You know he's not employed, right?" he asked, wishing his voice didn't sound so acidic. It wasn't any of his business anyway, which was exactly what Gwen said.

"I know that," he said, approaching her.

"*You're* the one who broke up with me," she said, her voice just as blunt and unforgiving as his.

"I know that," he repeated. He stopped in front of her, his nerves buzzing and his thoughts whirling. He couldn't tell her about Abby right this second. He couldn't kiss her. Gwen wasn't his to do anything with, and in fact, she could fire him without any explanation.

The fact that she hadn't revealed a lot about her and

her feelings for him, and Teagan was tired of pushing her away.

"Maybe I made a mistake," he said, pushing past her and entering the kitchen. "And now we're late for our meeting."

TEAGAN LEFT THE HEARTWOOD INN SEVERAL MINUTES after he normally did, having rushed through their specials of short ribs and rosemary and garlic mashed potatoes and the freshly caught halibut that had come off the boats that morning.

The prep team would have all the fillets ready, all the vegetables cut and seasoned, the desserts in the fridge before they left. Then he and his kitchen staff would come back and run their dinner service.

Teagan loved working in a busy kitchen, and Redfin was full most nights. The Heartwood Inn was full almost year-round, as the inn had a magical quality to it that even Teagan could feel.

"Dial Abby," he said to his Bluetooth speaker when he got home. His daughter might be in class as the fall semester of her junior year at Stanford had just started. Teagan wasn't privy to her entire schedule, and he didn't have any expectations as the line rang.

He wouldn't call her mother, because Caroline was sure to be working or sleeping. That was all the woman did, and Teagan had given up on communicating with her several years ago. The moment he'd bought his daughter a cell phone, in fact.

"Hey, Dad," Abby said, her voice bright and chipper.

"Not in class?" he asked.

"We just got out." She said something to someone with her in person, and Teagan waited. "All right. I have a couple of minutes. And you should know you interrupted me talking to a very cute guy."

"Oh, wow," Teagan chuckled. "This will just take a couple of minutes." He hoped. "I'm thinking of...there's this woman I like...."

Abby let a few seconds of silence go by, and then she said, "Dad, I didn't know you were a human," in a teasing voice. She laughed the moment she finished speaking, and Teagan laughed with her.

"Trust me," he said. "I am." He had plenty of flaws, just like anyone else. Probably more than other people, as he'd always put his work first. "Here's the thing. She's only thirty years old."

"I'm not sure I follow."

"You're only twenty, and...I don't know, is it weird for me to date a woman so close to your age?"

"I don't see why." She laughed again. "Dad, you've always worried so much about stuff."

"Have I?"

"Are you kidding?" Abby laughed again. "Remember when Mom got me that part on a movie set, and the filming was in the middle of the night? You worried about that, even though I was with Mom. And there was the time I was sixteen years old, and I wanted to go to a bonfire on the beach. From clear across the country, you worried that I'd get taken advantage of or burned or something."

"A father worries about his daughter," Teagan said. "That's called normal."

"Mom doesn't worry the way you do," she said.

"Well, your mother is a special kind of bird," Teagan said, and that was putting it kindly.

"She's an act-tress," Abby said in a fake British accent, dissolving into giggles again. "Dad, that cute guy is coming back. Listen, if you like this woman, go out with her. I'm not worried about the age thing."

"Okay," Teagan said, wishing he could be as carefree as his daughter. When he was her age, he was in a hospital with someone he'd just married, waiting to hear if their baby was a boy or a girl. "Good luck with the cute guy. What's his name?"

"Oh, I can't tell you that," Abby said. "It'll jinx my chances with him. Gotta go!" She hung up, and Teagan couldn't help shaking his head at his fun-loving daughter.

He fed his fish and turned around, his whole day in front of him. Back when he and Gwen were dating, they'd grab lunch together or go sit by the lighthouse and talk, sharing sodas and crackers and their lives.

"I miss her," he admitted to his empty house. Now that

he'd acknowledged his feelings for Gwen, he had to deal with them.

And he simply didn't know how—at least not in a way that wouldn't hurt her again. That was the worst part of seeing her every day, being so close to her. Knowing he'd hurt her gnawed at him until he could barely look at her, and the very idea of her going out with another man made his fingers clench.

So he just needed to find a way to look at her, apologize to her, and maybe get her to go out with *him*. That way, she wouldn't be going out with anyone else.

Oh, and he'd have to tell her about Abby if he truly wanted a second chance with her.

3

M*aybe I made a mistake.*

Teagan's words would not leave Gwen's mind, and dang if that didn't annoy her. It kept her from napping too, and she really needed to catch up on her sleep, as she'd been out late for a couple of nights this week.

The restaurant didn't care about her dating habits, and she still had to be to work by five o'clock in the morning, whether she'd taken a moonlit stroll on the beach or gone to bed by eight. Not that she went to bed by eight...okay, fine, she did try to be to bed by eight most nights.

But she'd been out with Daniel twice this week already, and she seriously needed a nap before tonight's dinner service. Though September had arrived on the island of Carter's Cove, The Heartwood Inn was still booked full, and that meant Redfin was too.

In fact, reservations were highly recommended on the weekends for the restaurant.

Maybe I made a mistake.

Those blasted words had Gwen turning over *again*, and she finally just sat up and put her legs over the edge of the bed. She couldn't believe Teagan was disrupting her sleep patterns. She'd thought she'd at least moved past that.

His disdain of Daniel had been obvious, even before he opened his mouth. And oh, what a mouth. Gwen sighed, and she couldn't decide if the sound was filled with longing or disgust. Probably both.

No, Daniel didn't have a job right now. Everyone fell on hard times, didn't they? Of course they did. But there were dozens of opportunities for work on Carter's Cove, as the tourism industry always needed more people. But Daniel hadn't had a job in several months....

Gwen pushed Teagan's implications away. It wasn't any of his business who she spent her time with, as he'd made it very clear he didn't want it to be with him.

She reached over and stroked Celeste's dog, Midnight, the little black pup such a good friend for Gwen. She never had to sleep alone if she didn't want to, and the dog would follow her around the house as if she didn't want to be alone either.

Not only that, but Celeste had inherited another dog from her boyfriend, Brad. The mutt was much bigger than Midnight, but Joey was very sweet, and it turned out he liked to lay around as much as he liked to chase a ball down the beach.

Gwent positioned a visor on her head and reached for Midnight's collar on her nightstand. "Let's go outside, guys."

Midnight jumped around, obviously eager to put her collar on and go. Gwen giggled at her as she struggled with the squirmy small dog, finally clicking the collar into position. "Get a ball, Joey."

The bigger canine just cocked his head and looked at her, obviously still learning a few English words. "Ball," Gwen repeated, knowing she'd end up finding the bright orange ball Joey liked so much.

She filled a water bottle with ice and water, grabbed the dog bowl from its spot near the back door, and looked around for a ball. Spying one by the couch, she'd taken a couple of steps toward it when Joey seemed to catch on. He lunged for the ball and scooped it up into his mouth.

"Good boy," she said. "Now drop it. Drop it."

Joey held onto the ball, his doggy smile indicating that he was just so proud of himself for finding the ball.

"Okay," Gwen said. "But if you want me to throw it, you'll have to drop it." She grabbed the throwing stick and a bag of dried liver treats and headed for the back door. Midnight and Joey raced through it first, wagging their tails as they waited for her to exit too, and then get the door on the screened-in back porch too.

She did, and they all tumbled down the steps to the

little bit of grass in the small backyard. "Drop it," Gwen said again, this time reaching into the bag for a dog treat. That got Joey to obey, and she picked up the ball with the throwing stick. She launched it out into the sand, and Joey and Midnight took off after it.

Sometimes Midnight would manage to get the ball before Joey—she was surprisingly fast for her small size—but she couldn't bring it back very well. So it was almost always Joey who brought the ball back to Gwen, dropped it, and sat waiting for his reward. Midnight got a treat too, so she always came right back to Gwen's feet on the edge of the grass.

Then Gwen would pick up the ball again, wipe the excess sand on the grass, and throw it again.

The September sun was as hot as the August sun, and Gwen only stayed out for twenty minutes, throwing the ball and enjoying the dogs. They slurped the ice water she brought out, and when she said, "Let's go in," they trotted ahead of her with sandy dog beards she'd wipe on the porch before letting them into the house.

As she was bent over wiping the sand off of Midnight's face, her phone chimed in her back pocket. The message better not be about some problem at the restaurant, or Gwen didn't know what she'd do.

Before she pulled her phone out and looked at it, she pressed her eyes closed. She needed a break from the restaurant, the catering, the special events, the beachside food service, the room service, all of it. Problem was, she didn't know how to take one.

When she looked at her phone, the message was from Teagan.

So definitely a problem.

But she couldn't stop herself from reading it. *I'm sorry about what I said earlier about your boyfriend. It really isn't my business.*

Gwen felt like there should be a but after the message, with another one coming any moment now. But her phone stayed silent. "What does he expect me to say to that?" she wondered. She could pretend she hadn't gotten it. For all he knew, she'd blocked his number when he'd cut her out of his life. Well, at least his personal life.

She wanted to know what he meant by the mistake comment, so she quickly tapped out a response to him. He could say what he wanted to her. Text her when he knew she napped during the day sometimes. Glare at her when she tried to help him in the kitchen.

She could ask him what he meant by something he'd said.

What did you mean by you might have made a mistake?

"Come on, guys," she said, realizing both dogs were crowding the door, trying to get it open while she texted. She opened the back door, and they all went inside where the blessed air conditioner worked really well.

Her phone spit out several notifications in a row, and

Gwen hurried to put the water bottle and dog bowl in the sink so she could read her messages more easily.

I meant I miss you.

I meant Daniel is nowhere good enough for you.

I meant I know I'm not either.

And I meant maybe I'd like to try again with you.

The breath left Gwen's body, and she looked up and out the window above the sink. Her heart beat in her chest in an irregular way, bouncing around as she tried to make sense of Teagan's texts.

Her phone buzzed, and she looked down.

I'm stupid for saying all this in a text.

Maybe we could go grab something to eat? Neither of us is asleep, obviously.

Gwen wanted to say yes. Badly. She also needed to pull back and be cool. Not rush into a heated romance with the man for a second time. But everything about Teagan made her want to stomp on the accelerator, from his beautiful eyes, to his devilish smile, to his olive skin.

And his mad skills in the kitchen. And his confidence. And he could be fun and flirty and amazing when he let his guard down. The Teagan in the kitchen had attracted her to him. But she'd fallen for the man he was outside the kitchen.

"Not again," she told herself. "At least not so fast." She spun around and found the dogs flopped on the floor by the air vent, panting. "I'm going out, guys," she said. "Don't tell Celeste."

All right, she tapped into her text messages as she hurried down the hall. She hadn't showered yet today, and she didn't want to go out with Teagan still smelling like hollandaise sauce. *I need forty-five minutes.*

I'll pick you up then, he said, and Gwen stepped into the shower, unable to stop the giddiness prancing through her.

AN HOUR LATER, GWEN CAME OUT OF HER BEDROOM AND walked her sandaled feet down the hall. Teagan had been sitting on her couch with the dogs for fifteen minutes, but she didn't care. He could wait for her. She'd been ready on time, but it had taken the past fifteen minutes to psyche herself up enough to leave her bedroom.

"I can't believe I'm doing this," she said, and he rose from the couch.

Several feet separated them, and Gwen felt like his eyes possessed a traction ray. She couldn't move, and she couldn't look away.

"I'm sorry," he said, clearing his throat. The sound broke the traction ray's power over her, and she shuffled her feet and looked away. "I know I owe you an explanation, and I want to give it. I do. I just...."

Gwen wanted to hear him talk in that smooth, whole voice he had. The tonalities of it could reach right into her heart and pluck all the right strings.

"Where do you want to eat?" Gwen asked at the same time Teagan said, "I have a daughter."

Gwen's gaze flew back to Teagan's, pure surprise rendering her mute. Her eyebrows went up as if they had a mind all their own, and she didn't remember telling her voice to say, "A daughter?" but she definitely did.

Teagan's eyes stormed, and his jaw clenched, and Gwen was so darn happy that he was there, standing in front of her and talking.

Well, at least he had been talking. Now he just looked like he wanted to punch something.

4

Teagan needed to get his emotions under wraps before he could say anything else.

"I didn't realize you'd been married," Gwen said, and her voice was soft and gentle, a clear invitation for him to keep talking.

"Once," he said, his muscles releasing the slightest bit. "A long time ago. A very long time ago." He wanted to sigh and pinch the bridge of his nose. He did neither but watched Gwen devour him with those clear, deep blue eyes.

"My daughter is twenty years old," he said. "She lives in California near her mother. I was...I got all worked up over your age. And her age." He did sigh then, collapsing back onto the couch. This wasn't how he'd envisioned telling Gwen about Abby. He'd planned to take her to Last Course, a semi-fancy dessert restaurant on the island that only served the last course of a meal. He knew she loved that place, and if he could get her eating a brownie bomb, maybe it wouldn't be so hard to tell her about his past.

Gwen sat beside him on the couch, perfectly silent. She reached over and brushed his longish hair back out of his eyes, and then laced her hand through his. Sparks buzzed through his skin, his bones, up his arm, infecting his brain. Her touch felt so, so good.

He stared at her face, but she dropped her gaze to their intertwined fingers. "You get too far inside your head sometimes," she finally said.

"That's what Abby said. She's my daughter." Now that the secret was out, Teagan wasn't sure why he'd clung so hard to it. "Does that...I mean, I'm sure it does. But does she change things for you?"

"What things?" Gwen looked up, and their eyes met.

"Things between us."

Gwen swallowed, her eyes rounding slightly as a hint of fear entered them. "I want things to change between us, Teagan. What's been going on isn't...."

"Isn't what?" he prompted.

"It isn't what I want," she said. "I know this isn't a secret to you."

"What isn't?"

She rolled her eyes then. "You aren't this stupid." Gwen got up and walked away, putting furniture and a partial wall between them as she moved into the kitchen and turned on the sink. She filled a glass with water, her back to him, and drank.

A clunk sounded in her house as she set the glass in the sink, and she didn't face him as she said, "I've had feelings for you since the day we met, Teagan. They didn't go away after you broke up with me."

Teagan stood, feeling foolish and out of his league when it came to Gwen. She had this uncanny ability to say what she felt and thought in such a clear, concise way. He always felt like he was floundering in the dark when it came to how he felt. And articulating it? Running a busy kitchen was easier.

He ground his voice through his throat again. "Mine didn't go away either," he said, and that got Gwen to turn around.

"I want pizza for lunch," she said. "And then a lot of dessert."

Teagan grinned at her. "Pizza and then we'll go by Last Course." He cocked his elbow for her, and she strode across the space between them and slipped her arm through his.

"I'm ordering a ton of chocolate," she said. "So be ready."

Teagan chuckled, ducked his head, and thanked the stars above for his good luck—and Gwen's willingness to try again.

Now he just had to make sure he didn't mess up for a second time.

TEAGAN DID NOT SUGGEST THEY SHARE AT PIE SQUARED, though they certainly didn't need two pizzas between them. But he wanted the Low Country barbecue chicken pizza, which came with braised collard greens, fresh tomatoes, and slivered red onions, and he knew she wouldn't eat that.

So he let her step up to the counter and order a pepperoni pizza with olives on thin crust—literally everything he disliked—and then he ordered what he wanted. The short drive over from her house had been mostly him apologizing for the radio not working and asking Gwen how her mom and dad were doing now that they were fully retired.

"Great," she'd said. "Dad fishes a lot, and Mom's busy making sure my grandmother doesn't break another hip." She'd smiled while she said it, but Teagan felt like there was still a wide chasm between them, and he didn't know how to build a bridge across it.

"Drinks?" the waitress asked, and Teagan ordered Coke while he waited for Gwen to ask for a flavored lemonade.

When she said, "I'll have Coke too," he gaped at her.

The waitress walked away before he said, "Coke? I didn't think you liked cola."

"People change," she said, her voice definitely holding some cool notes. "Tell me about your wife."

"Ex-wife," he said quickly. "You know her. I mean, you don't *know* her, but I'm sure you've heard of her." He hated telling people he'd been married to Caroline Faye. Maybe that was why he never did.

Literally, ever.

Teagan worked a lot, and he had very few friends outside of the kitchen. Those he did have didn't need to know about a marriage that had ended almost twenty years ago.

He looked at Gwen, pure vulnerability flowing through him and making him swallow. "Caroline Faye," he said, ready to say her response with her.

The actress?

"The actress?" she asked, and Teagan wanted to roll his eyes. He'd hoped Gwen's reaction would be different than everyone else's.

"Yes," he said, pulling his water glass closer to him so he'd have something to focus on. "We were married for eleven months. She had Abby after the divorce, and I'd already left the state. I was twenty years old."

And he'd have done so many things differently if he could. But at twenty, he'd done what he'd been capable of at the time, and that wasn't to go back to a state he hated and be a father.

He watched Gwen, sure she'd make a quip about how he'd abandoned his daughter and demand to know how he could do something like that. At the same time, Gwen wasn't a cruel person, and maybe Teagan had some unresolved issues that lived inside him that he needed to deal with.

"I'll bet you missed her," she said, and Teagan didn't know what to do with that.

"I did," he said. "There were so many things I regret missing." So, so many. But Caroline didn't really raise Abby either, and Teagan had been sending money for years—not that Caroline needed it.

"You can't live your whole life with regret," she said.

"Actually," Teagan said, though he knew when he started sentences like that, Gwen's annoyance shot through the roof. "You can. I have."

"Teagan." She cocked her head at him as if trying to figure him out, and Teagan loved it. She was so cute, and so kind, and he wished he could explain himself to her in a way that made sense. But, well, it didn't make sense inside his own mind, so how could she possibly understand?

Their drinks arrived, and Gwen busied herself with unwrapping her straw. "Have you really lived your whole life with regret?"

"Did you hear all the stuff I've just told you?" He wasn't proud of any of it, and not a day went by that he didn't think of Abby, where he didn't imagine how different his life would be now if he'd made different decisions then.

"Anyway," he said when she didn't answer. "I tell myself I've done the best I could. I have a decent relationship with my daughter." He put his straw in his drink too and took a long pull, the sugary cola calming his nerves immediately. "In fact, Abby was the one who told me to get over myself and call you if I liked you."

Gwen looked up from her soda, the straw still swirling, swirling, swirling around. She gazed at him, utterly calm as she asked, "And do you? Like me?"

"Yes," Teagan said. "Yes, I do."

A smile touched her lips, and Teagan dropped his eyes to her mouth, wondering what it would be like to finally kiss her. That was a step they'd never taken last time they were together, and in fact, he'd broken up with her on the very night he should've kissed her.

Walked her right up to her front door—and said, "I don't think we should see each other anymore," when he should've pressed her into the door and kissed her like she was his.

"Good," she said. "Because I kinda like you, too."

5

Gwen could not believe she'd just told Teagan right to his face that she liked him. She'd spent the last six months pretending like she didn't. Worse, even. Pretending like she actually *dis*liked him.

"Pepperoni with olives," the waitress said. "Low Country Greens." She set the two pizzas down, and the tension between her and Teagan broke.

She admired her pizza, and then his, and said, "We should do something like this for events."

"No work talk," he said, picking up a piece of his pizza. "That was a rule last time, and I actually really liked it."

Gwen hadn't, but she didn't argue. "Okay," she said, because yeah, maybe she didn't need to talk about work all the time. But she enjoyed talking about it with Teagan, because he was her equal. He knew as much as she did about The Heartwood Inn kitchens, the workload, the burden, the joy, the fun. His skills in the kitchen were only matched by hers, and she wanted to share that with him.

"I would like to cook with you again," he said, and he took a bite of his pizza.

Pure heat flowed through Gwen's veins like lava moving down a volcano. "All right," she said as coolly as she could.

"Your place?" he asked. "Sunday afternoon?"

"You're going to take my Sunday afternoon nap from me?" she teased.

He simply grinned at her, took another bite of his pizza, and waited.

Gwen made him wait too, and then she finally said, "And I think your place would be better. Celeste will ask too many questions, and she doesn't work on Sundays."

"My place it is," he said, running one hand through that delicious long hair that Gwen really wanted to fist in her fingers as she kissed him.

She couldn't believe she was already thinking about kissing him. But truth be told, she'd been thinking about it for months and months, because she'd never actually done it. They'd been close last time, and Gwen really hoped something else didn't come up to drive Teagan away again. She wasn't sure her heart could stand the turmoil, the up and down, the yes and then no.

After all, she knew what it felt like to live with a

broken heart, and she didn't want to spend her life doing that.

THAT NIGHT IN THE KITCHEN, THE ATMOSPHERE WAS completely different. Everyone felt it, and Gordon looked between Gwen and Teagan like he knew they'd been out that afternoon. Shared a bit of their lives with each other. Made another date. Held hands in the car and then on the walk up to her front door.

She hadn't lingered on the porch for a kiss, because her anxiety over what had happened last time on that porch had practically shoved her into the house. Celeste hadn't been home—not surprising—and Gwen had showered and actually put a little bit of makeup on before returning to the inn.

She wasn't sure why she'd done that. She felt like everyone was staring at her while Teagan went over the menu for that evening, set the specials with the waitresses, and assigned stations.

Gwen didn't normally stay for the entire dinner service. Some nights, she put on posh clothes and walked the dining room floor with Bea, her front-of-house manager. She chatted with guests and helped clean tables and watched their seating procedures.

She almost always left by eight or nine, retreating back to the house on the beach and the screened-in porch, where she usually fell asleep until Celeste came to wake her. Of course, Celeste had been staying out later and later with her new boyfriend, and their system had been working well.

Some nights—like tonight—Gwen would tie an apron around her waist and make sure Teagan knew she wanted to cook. She hadn't spent years in New York City at one of the best culinary institutes in the country to oversee meal prep.

"Gwen," he said, drawing her out of her mind. "You're on desserts."

She nodded, though she also inwardly groaned. The dessert station meant she would be here all night long, right up until the restaurant closed so she could serve the last customer the chocolate mousse they wanted.

At the same time, a measure of excitement moved through her. She and Teagan would be here late tonight, and she turned away from him as the meeting broke up before he could see her smile. Maybe he'd send everyone else home quickly, and she could kiss him in the kitchen.

Nope, she told herself as she moved over to the dessert station with a talented pastry chef named Lauren Mitchell. The two women nodded to each other, and Lauren put the one-sheet of desserts for that night's menu on the counter in front of them.

They were offering four selections that night, including drunk peach pie—which Gwen wanted a piece of right that moment—chocolate tuxedo cake with ganache and a dark chocolate mousse, a caramel blondie with peach ice cream, and a raspberry souffle. The last one would be the hardest, so Gwen didn't argue when Lauren said, "I'll take the souffles and the blondies, if that's okay."

"Absolutely fine," she said. The peach pie was easy. Slice, plate, sprinkle with cinnamon sugar. The tuxedo cake was more involved, simply because of the canneles she'd need to make for the mousse. She surveyed the prep station in front of her, went into the refrigeration unit specifically for desserts and noted how many servings of each item they had, and had just returned to the kitchen when Teagan said, "All right, everyone. First order is in." He read off a tablet propped in front of him. "Dessert first for table thirteen. Tuxedo cake and raspberry souffle."

"Yes, chef," Gwen and Lauren recited back to him simultaneously, and they were off the ground and running already.

"Fire scallops and bruschetta," he said to the appetizer team. "And we've got two specials."

The kitchen moved like the well-oiled machine it had become, and Gwen couldn't help the tingle of excitement moving through her. There was nothing as amazing as working in a five-star kitchen, with a chef who knew how to get the results he wanted with the food and still maintain friendships with his chefs.

The dinner service passed quickly, much to Gwen's surprise. She felt like she should be exhausted, but as she started combining chocolate sauces into one bottle so the rest could be washed, she felt alive and ready for the next thing the night held.

"You can go, Lauren," Teagan said, and Gwen used every ounce of her self-control not to look up. "Thanks for a great night."

Lauren said something to him too, but Gwen didn't hear what. She was maybe five minutes away from being finished and cleaned up too, and she capped the chocolate sauce just as the kitchen door slammed.

"Almost done?" Teagan asked, turning toward her.

"Yes, chef," she said. "Just a few more dishes."

He chuckled, the deep, sexy sound of it making Gwen's cheeks flame as she walked into the fridge and put her chocolate sauce away. She took a deep breath. Teagan had been brave to text her and tell her things he hadn't wanted to tell her before. In fact, he'd said things that had caused him to break up with her before.

"You want to kiss him," she said, starting to get a chill in the refrigeration unit. "So just do it." She wasn't sure if she wanted her first kiss with the man to happen in the industrial kitchen at the inn or not. It wasn't a terribly romantic spot, what with all the glinting steel, scent of onions hanging in the air, and the bright fluorescent lights.

She felt sweaty and sticky, and her chef's jacket didn't make her feel desirable or sexy. She loosened the buttons and let it hang open before returning to the kitchen.

Teagan had finished wiping down her station for her, his jacket gone completely. He wore a blue T-shirt that seemed fresh from the dryer, and he really was the most breathtaking man Gwen had ever laid eyes on.

"Done," he said, smiling at her.

"Thanks," she said. "I'm definitely going to need a nap tomorrow."

"Me too," he said. "Because we have to be back here in six hours."

A sigh passed through Gwen as she thought of it, and she groaned. "Don't remind me." She approached him, her heartbeat turning into booms in her chest. He received her easily and willingly into his arms, and once again, Gwen felt anything but tired.

"It was a good service," she said, immediately regretting the words.

"Yeah." He played with the end of her ponytail, which sent shivers down her back and across her shoulders.

She looked up at him, making a quick decision she hoped she wouldn't regret. Tipping up onto her toes, she closed her eyes and brushed her mouth against his.

"Oh." He flinched away from her, clearly surprised.

"Sorry," she muttered, pure humiliation pulling through her.

"Don't be sorry," he said, one hand sliding behind her neck and bringing her closer again. He kissed her then, a sensual, slow kiss that felt like he'd been thinking about kissing her for six months too.

He held her in place, kissing her and kissing her and kissing her, until the heat in Gwen's body screamed at her to take a breath, pull away, cool down.

She didn't, because kissing Teagan in real life was so much better than even her fantasies had imagined.

6

Teagan could not stop kissing Gwen Heartwood. Her lips were full and smooth and utterly delicious, almost like she'd swiped a bit of that chocolate sauce on them before coming out of the refrigeration unit.

He knew he was holding her too close. Kissing her too deeply and too long. Showing too much of how he felt.

He simply didn't care. He'd wanted this woman for as long as he could remember, and he'd finally gotten out of his own way enough to have a shot with her. She had her hands in his hair, and then along the sides of his face, and then clutching his shoulders like she might fall without having something to anchor herself to.

He threaded his hands through her hair, moving one down her back to her waist, where he pressed her closer to him. She couldn't get close enough.

He wasn't sure if she broke the connection or he did,

but the kiss ended, leaving him wanting more though he'd certainly taken enough from her. His ragged breathing matched hers, thankfully, and she leaned her forehead against his shoulder for a moment.

"Wow," she whispered, and Teagan couldn't have articulated anything better.

Gwen looked up at him, those blue eyes wide and open and vulnerable. Teagan didn't try to mask anything, maybe for the first time in his life. He simply let her look at him while he looked back at her.

He was tired from head to toe, but a new electricity zipped through his muscles, giving him a second wind. Or maybe a third wind. Sometime around the middle of dinner service, a wave of exhaustion had hit him. He'd left the kitchen for several minutes, asking Gordon to take over for him.

The other man had, of course, and the kitchen ran just fine under Gordon's hand. He'd watched the waves for a few minutes as the sun set behind the inn, and he'd yanked on the rejuvenation he needed to make it through the rest of the night.

But kissing Gwen had probably just ensured he wouldn't sleep that night.

"We should go," she finally said, and Teagan blinked.

"Yeah, just one more thing first." He dipped his head and kissed her again, because just as he'd suspected, kissing Gwen Heartwood was life-changing, and he wanted to do it again and again and again.

SUNDAY MORNING FOUND TEAGAN LEAVING THE INN AT THE same time he did every day. He would not be napping today, because Gwen was coming over. He'd seen her at work, of course, but he hadn't really been alone with her since the kiss on Friday night.

Fine, yesterday she'd called him into her office "to chat," but she'd said nothing before kissing him. He really liked that she seemed to be thinking about him as much as he did her, and she'd said, "We're still cooking together tomorrow, right?" as he held her close.

"Yes," he confirmed.

And now that time had come. He swung by the grocery store to get the ingredients he wanted for the noodle soup he had in mind. Yes, it was still very much summer on the island of Carter's Cove, but he loved oriental soups, and he knew Gwen did too.

A sense of comfort descended on him as he placed item after item in his shopping cart. He hadn't felt this... peaceful in months. Years. Maybe ever. Teagan always felt like he was running from something, hiding something, boxing something up tight so he didn't have to think about it. Explain it.

But he'd told Gwen about his former marriage and daughter and she hadn't judged him. She'd said very little about it, actually, and Teagan wasn't sure what to make of it. Surely, she had feelings about the man he'd been.

Or maybe she just wants to know about that man, and the one you are now.

Teagan paused, the thought moving through his head slowly again. He wasn't the same man he'd been twenty years ago when he'd met Caroline Faye. Or the same person he'd been when he'd left. Or even the same man he'd been a few days ago.

That was Teagan Hatch, the man who was afraid of losing what he didn't even have yet. And now that he had Gwen in his life, he wanted to keep her there.

He turned the corner, the ice cream aisle spreading before him. He loved sweets, but he wanted them to be balanced. The local grocery store here made a variety of specialty ice creams, and he paused to carefully consider them.

In the end, he selected green tea ice cream and pistachio, thinking they'd both pair well with the soup on his menu. At home, he unloaded everything and opened the back door to let in the breeze. He didn't live on the beach or even that close to it, but he supposed everywhere on Carter's Cove could be considered near the beach.

His apartment was on the top floor of the tallest building the island City Council would approve. Eight stories, and he had a great view of the east and west coastlines. On a clear day, he could see the mainland from his front porch, and if he opened his bathroom window, he had a perfect view of the lighthouse.

He spent very little time at home, but he did enjoy his

space. He couldn't remember the last time he'd cleaned, so he quickly wiped down the guest bathroom and had just gotten all of the groceries put away when Gwen knocked on his front door.

His pulse bobbed in the back of his throat, and any thoughts of changing his clothes real quick flew from his mind. Hurrying to the door, he told himself to *calm down. Act cool. Be normal.*

Problem was, he wasn't sure what Gwen's definition of normal was.

She stood on his front porch, her arms full of three bags of groceries. "Whoa," he said instead of hello. "Let me help you." He reached for the bags, and she willingly passed over two of them.

"I told you I'd get the stuff for soup, right?" he asked, backing up and drinking in the sight of her. She wore a pair of cutoffs that showed way more leg than Teagan had seen on her, ever. In addition to that, she wore a cute blouse that tied in a knot right over her belly button, the black stripes crossing the fabric and making alternating orange and white stripes.

In short, she was absolutely beautiful, and Teagan couldn't even remember what he'd asked her.

She said something as she stepped past him, but the scent of lemons and roses distracted him, as did the way her hair fell over her shoulders in delicious waves. Having enough awareness to close the door took all his energy, but he got it done.

He turned back to her just as she set her bag of groceries on the counter in his kitchen. How many times had he envisioned her here? So many.

Teagan swallowed and followed her, putting down the rest of the things she'd brought. "So I thought I'd do a vegetable tempura," she said, pulling out asparagus and zucchini squash. "That'll go well with the soup, right?"

"Absolutely," he said.

"I got prawns," she said, producing them. "And I may have started getting ideas about dessert." She looked up at him, a package of dark chocolate in one hand and a carton of cream in the other. Her blue eyes sparkled at him like sapphires, and he realized she was flirting with him.

He grinned at her, ready to play this game with her until he could press her right against the kitchen counter and kiss her. "Whatever you have in mind for dessert is fine with me."

"Are you sure?"

Teagan thought of the ice cream in his freezer. She didn't need to know about it. "Of course."

"I find it hard to believe you didn't plan something for dessert."

"Well, believe it."

Gwen rolled her eyes, an action she'd done dozens of times over the past six months. But this time, it felt playful instead of angry, and Teagan chuckled as he helped her unpack her groceries.

Surveying the ingredients she'd brought, he started to see where she was going. "Cake or cookies?" he asked.

"Cake, of course," she said. "Ten-year-olds make cookies."

"Hey, I had these cookies on the mainland last week that were *amazing*."

Gwen folded up her reusable grocery bags and tucked them between his toaster and his refrigerator as if she lived here. Suddenly, Teagan needed to nudge down the air conditioner and close that back door. He always opened it, because he liked the scent of the sea air, the sound of the street noise below him, and the amazing island breeze that came bustling in from time to time.

But standing with Gwen in his kitchen, her eyes on him and the thought of cooking with her, and Teagan needed a cold drink and something to get his internal temperature back to normal.

"You'll have to take me there," Gwen said.

Teagan's mind blanked. "Where?"

She giggled and ducked her head, and that only made his desire for her shoot through the roof. She was powerful and confident in the kitchen at The Heartwood Inn, and he really liked her in that environment.

Buttoned up in a chef's jacket, with her hair slicked back, her notes in front of her, and kind strength pouring from her.

But he liked this more feminine, fun, flirty version of the woman too, and he hoped he'd get to see more of her.

"The cookie place," she said, stepping into his personal space. She slowly—oh, so slowly—slid her hands up his arms and tipped up onto her toes. His eyes drifted closed as if she'd kiss him, but instead she said, "All right, chef. Let's cook."

Teagan could wait to kiss her. He felt like he'd earned a PhD in Waiting to Kiss Gwen Heartwood. So if she wanted to cook, he could wait a bit longer—and he'd cook.

7

Gwen tied an apron around her waist, her body's cue to stop flirting and get to work. Flirting with Teagan was a lot of fun, though, as he seemed to lose his train of thought really easily.

"So," she said, exhaling as she started unboxing the unsalted butter. "Have you dated a lot since your marriage ended?"

Teagan made a choking noise, and she turned in time to see him drop the bundle of celery in his arms. He carried at least half a dozen vegetables, and he stepped over to the island and dumped them there.

"I suppose—no. Not much."

Gwen nodded at him and turned to survey his cabinets. "Do you have a stand mixer? If not, it's—"

"Right here." Teagan practically tripped over his own

feet to get to a cupboard directly in front of her. He bent and opened it, pulling out the mixer she'd requested.

Gwen found his nerves cute, but she really wanted him to settle down and cook. Be real with her. Just talk while they put some delicious food together. She ignored the mixer for a moment and stood next to him. "Tell me about your soup."

"It's not a traditional pho," he said. "But it starts off that way." As he started telling her about the ingredients and why he put them in the noodle soup, he relaxed. Satisfaction pulled through Gwen, and she got back to putting together her batter too.

He finished talking at the same time he finished chopping the onion, and it hit the hot oil in the Dutch oven on his stovetop in the next moment. The scent of hot oil and onions filled the air, and Gwen basked in the sizzling sound of it.

"How do you feel about pets?" she asked.

"If I didn't work so much, I'd have one," he said.

"Traditional, like a dog or a cat? Or are we talking exotic?"

"Exotic?" He laughed then, the sound full and throaty. "Are goldfish exotic?"

"I wouldn't think so." She smiled as she greased a cake pan.

"Lizards?"

"Nope."

"Ferrets?"

"I'm not even sure I know what a ferret is."

He chuckled again as he worked from the cutting board to the pot, adding spices and ginger, baby corn cobs, and bok choy. "Probably just a dog or a cat," he said. "In fact, probably a cat. Then I don't have to exercise them."

"Mm, wise choice," Gwen said, getting back to her own recipe. She wasn't entirely sure where she was, because watching Teagan cook was so interesting. So hot.

She cleared her throat and focused. She didn't want her cake to be a flop.

"Let's go back to the dating question," Teagan said, easily now. "Do you date a lot?"

Gwen laughed, sure he was joking. "Not even a little bit."

"Really? Seems like you've been out with a few men lately."

Gwen paused again, this time cutting a look at him out of the corner of her eye. "Were you watching me?"

"Wasn't that obvious?" he asked, grinning at her as he stepped over to the sink for water.

She supposed it was. "I...haven't had much luck with men." She nodded. That summed things up nicely.

"What do you want?" he asked.

"I'm sorry?"

"What do you want your life to be?"

"I thought we were talking about dating."

"We were. I just moved us to this. Dating is part of your life, right?"

Gwen nodded, because yes, it was. "I want...I want my life to be about more than the inn." As soon as the words left her mouth, Gwen wished she could pull them back in. There were too many feelings inside those words. Too many revelations. Too many answers she didn't know.

"That's interesting," Teagan said.

"What about you?" she asked. "What do you want your life to be?"

"My life is what I want it to be," he said.

"Really?" she asked. "You have everything you want, right now."

He shrugged, stirring everything together. He put the lid on his Dutch oven and adjusted the flame underneath it before turning toward her. "I mean, I'm here with you, cooking in my house. So yeah, right here, right now, I have everything I want."

Gwen felt like she'd been backed into a corner. Her answer had opened so many doors she wished she'd kept closed. "If we're doing right here, right now, in this moment, anyone could say that."

"True," he said, leaning against the counter and folding his arms. The action made his biceps bigger, and Gwen turned away from the handsome sight of him in that white T-shirt.

"What more do you want besides the inn?" he asked.

"Nothing," Gwen said, swallowing. She poured her cake batter into the pans and turned to put them in the oven. Teagan's eyes on the side of her face felt so heavy, but she refused to look at him.

"Come on, Gwenny," he said, almost teasing.

She faced him, her pulse bumping a little harder than it had been a moment ago. "You have to tell me something real if you want me to share something real with you."

"I did," he said. "I told you things about my past I haven't told very many people."

"How many people?" she asked, feeling some of the challenge spark back to life inside her.

"My sister," he said. "My mother."

"No father?"

"My father passed away when I was very young," he said. "Five or six."

Regret stained Gwen's heart immediately. "I'm so sorry."

"I don't remember him," Teagan said. "I mean, sometimes I feel like I knew him, but then...." He paused, looking somewhere inside his mind. "Then the moment passes."

"And where are your mom and sister?"

"Whistlestop Shores," he said, turning to open the fridge so she couldn't see his face. She couldn't tell from the tone of his voice how he felt about that.

"Are you from there?"

"Yes, ma'am," he said. "Born and raised." He straightened, the carton of cream in his hand. "Want me to help with this?"

"No, sir," she said, taking the cream and putting it back in the fridge. This dance with him in the kitchen was fun, and easy, and she was glad she didn't have to avoid him the way she'd been doing.

"So your family must be wealthy," she said.

"My mother came from money," he said evasively, and Gwen started thinking through any famous Hatch's she knew. But she'd never been one to run in high society circles, though her family had plenty of money too.

"Will you take me to Whistlestop Shores?" she asked, moving some of her dishes into the kitchen sink. He joined her there, and it was very nice to work side-by-side with him.

"Sure," he said. "It's a great place."

"I've been a few times," she said. "But not for a while."

"I'll give you the locals tour." He grinned at her and turned on the hot water.

Gwen swirled her hands in the water as he added soap, and he put his in too. He took her hand and squeezed, and she stilled, letting the perfectness of the moment wash over her.

"I haven't forgotten that you didn't tell me what you wanted outside of the inn," he said, his voice much quieter now.

A flash of irritation moved through her. "I shouldn't have said that. I have a good life."

"Of course you do," he said gently. This softer side of

him was nice, but Gwen also didn't know what to do with it. "But it's okay to want more too."

Gwen did want more. She wanted some days off. She wanted a partner in her life that wasn't her sister. She loved Celeste, but she and Brad would get engaged and then married, and Gwen would still have the family house on the beach and the kitchen at the inn.

She wanted a family, but she absolutely wasn't telling Teagan that. At least not right now, on this, essentially their second date.

"Maybe you'll tell me one day," he said.

"Sure," she said, her way of saying *Not today.*

Thankfully, Teagan left it at that, and Gwen appreciated that gesture. "So the grand opening of the VIP pool is on Tuesday," she said. "Do you want to go with me?"

"Sure," Teagan said, absolutely no hesitation in his voice. Warmth and happiness moved through Gwen, and she enjoyed the rest of her afternoon with the most handsome—and most talented—chef on the island.

"I HAVE CAKE," GWEN SAID AS SHE ENTERED HER PARENTS' house.

"Cake?" Her dad sat up from where he'd been reclining in the couch. "I want cake." He put the leg rest down and stood up.

Gwen accepted a quick side-hug from her dad and

handed the cake to him with a smile. "It's a black and white cake, Pops."

"Looks amazing." He grinned at her and took the cake she'd made at Teagan's into the kitchen, where her grandmother waited with a knife.

"I'll put coffee on," her mom said, and the bustling and hustling in the kitchen warmed Gwen's heart. She was exhausted, and she still needed to get back over to the restaurant for their dinner service. She wasn't working the kitchen that night, but Bea had a family affair starting at eight, and Gwen would take over the floor then.

"How's the kitchen?" her dad asked, and Gwen sighed.

"Dad, did you ever just want a day off? Or a week?"

He looked up, concern instantly in his dark blue eyes. Her mother had all the light blonde, blue-eyed genes, and every one of Gwen's sisters had a shade of blue eyes and a shade of blonde hair.

Gwen's was quite light in all areas, and she'd always wished she had hair that didn't wisp away like cornsilk and eyes that didn't look like someone made a mistake by not putting in enough dye.

"You look tired, dear," her mom said, and Gwen sighed again.

"Thanks, Mom."

"Gwenny," her dad said, actually abandoning the cake and coming back toward her. He took her by both shoulders, his big hands so comforting and kind. "If you need a break, you take one. Always."

"But the kitchen—"

"The kitchen will be there when you get back," he said, peering down at her. "I mean it. The only way, and I mean the *only* way, I survived running that place was taking time when I needed it."

"And he never took enough," her mom said.

Gwen looked away, her emotions so close to the surface now. She loved her parents, and she was glad her dad hadn't blown her question away like it was nothing. "Okay," she said, her voice a bit shaky. "Then I need some time off."

"Then make the arrangements and take it." Her dad kept his gaze on her as he dropped his hands. "And listen, if you don't want the job you have, but you want to stay at the inn, talk to O. She'll find a good fit for you."

"And if you don't want to work at the inn at all, that's okay too," her mom said. "Right, Henry?"

"Of course," her dad said. "We've always said you girls could choose what you wanted to be. And you can be anything."

"Look at Alissa," Grams said from the kitchen. "She's got that shop now, and we ate her fish for lunch today."

Gwen smiled at her family, her eyes tearing up now. "Okay." She stepped into a full hug now, hoping to take a moment to calm herself so she didn't cry. "I think I'm okay in the kitchens for now."

Her mom smiled and patted her head like she was a

little dog, and then turned back to the kitchen. "Let's have a piece of this cake."

"Why did you make the cake, dear?" Grams asked, almost dropping the plates as she got them out of the cupboard.

"Mom," her mother said. "Go sit down. I've got this."

Grams didn't seem to notice the exasperation in her daughter-in-law's voice, and she merrily went to sit at the dining room table.

"Well," Gwen said. "I sort of have a new boyfriend, and we made the cake this afternoon together."

"A new boyfriend?" her mom exclaimed in a voice twice as loud as before.

"Oh, boy," her dad said, smiling as he turned to help with the cake.

"He's sort of an old boyfriend too," Gwen said, her smile fading. "I'm not really sure how things will go." But she was already kissing him, as if the last six months without Teagan had never happened.

"An old boyfriend too," Grams said. "Must be Teagan."

Her mother dropped the knife she was using to cut the cake. A horrible clattering sound filled the kitchen, along with her voice saying, "Teagan? Really?" just before her dad said, "Don't bleed all over the cake, Gladys."

8

Teagan couldn't believe how happy he was. He woke up without a pit of dread in his stomach, though it was four a.m. He arrived at the inn without tension in his shoulders. He worked with a smile way down in his soul, especially when Gwen came in, caught his eye, and smiled.

A rush of humiliation filled him each time that happened, but as one morning faded into another, that feeling started to lessen.

So he'd made a mistake. It wasn't his first one, by any means. "Now all you need to do is figure out how to not make another one," he muttered to himself. "Especially with Gwen."

"What?" Gordon asked, and Teagan startled in his meal prep for breakfast, which would begin in fifteen minutes.

"Nothing," Teagan said, heat rising to his face. Of course he knew he wasn't alone. He just forgot sometimes, as a chef sometimes really got deep into his own mind. "How's Kennedy?" Gordon had recently gotten married, and his wife was finishing up her beauty classes on the mainland.

"Doing real good," Gordon said in his Southern drawl. "She'll be done at the end of October, and she's starting to set up her shop."

"It'll be in your place at home, right?" Teagan asked. Gordon was really his only friend in the kitchen. Before Gordon had gotten married, he and Teagan had hung out a few times.

"That's right," he said with a smile. "How do you remember so many details about everyone you talk to?"

"Do I?" Teagan laughed and finished dicing the ham. He had a literal vat of it as their special today was the ham and cheese omelet, and he expected a lot of orders. Even kids liked ham and cheese in their eggs, and it was Tuesday, so kids ate free all day long.

"Yes, you do," Gordon said. "It's kind of creepy, and kind of cool." They laughed together, and then Margo came through the swinging plastic door.

"There's a line down the hall already," she said, wearing her stern front-of-the-house manager face. Teagan liked Margo just fine, but her dark-haired ponytail sometimes got a little too tight, and she got a little too wound up—especially on Tuesdays.

"So let's have our A-game on today," she said, sweeping her gaze across the chefs standing there. Besides Teagan and Gordon, there were four women who worked the breakfast shift, and two cooks doing prep work for lunch and dinner that Teagan could pull onto the line if necessary.

In addition to that, Gwen oversaw a team of six people who put together the room service orders for the inn, and those would continue to go out for three more hours.

And Gwen.

Oh, Gwen.

Teagan's mouth turned dry at the very thought of Gwen working in the kitchen, and he glanced toward her office door. She leaned against the doorjamb like her weight was needed to keep it upright. She had her arms folded over her T-shirt, which had a sparkly pineapple on it. She wore black slacks this morning, but Teagan didn't know why. Her roles at the inn were many and varied, and he wasn't even sure how she kept them all straight.

"Teagan?" Margo prompted, and he sure hoped it was the first time.

He stepped beside her and faced the group too. "It's Tuesday, guys, so nothing crazy. Specials are ham and cheese omelets, which Vivi will do, and a peach Belgian waffle that I'll man. And Gordon and I will take care of regular orders." He clapped his hands together. "All right?"

"Yes, chef," they chorused back to him, and a smidge

of foolishness ran through him. But he sure did like being called chef and having all of his orders obeyed.

All right, chef. Let's cook. Gwen's words to him on Sunday just before they got cooking in his kitchen ran through his mind.

He said, "All right. Then let's cook," with a quick glance in her direction.

Her eyes met his and held, and Teagan swore everything else in the huge, busy, industrial kitchen fell into silence. Into nothing. As fast as it had done that, everything came rushing back, and he stepped over to the Belgian waffle makers to double-check and make sure they were all on.

He had peaches coming out of his ears, as well as raspberries and strawberries prepped, as they often got requests for other fruits when the waffle was on special.

Margo stepped over to him, bringing the scent of something antiseptic with her. "All ready?" she asked, pressing far too close into him. She was more his age than Gwen's, but Teagan wasn't interested in Margo. And he'd told her that.

Maybe he needed to tell her he was back together with her boss. He said nothing and edged away from her. Of course he was ready. Hadn't she just heard him say *let's cook*?

Teagan probably could've dated more than he had over the years. Margo wasn't the first woman to let him know she'd like to go out with him. The fact that Gwen never had only added to the woman's allure, at least in Teagan's eyes. He liked being the one to ask a woman out. He liked picking her up at her place, and he liked making the first move.

With Gwen, she did all of those things too, and he didn't mind. She'd kissed him in the kitchen last Friday night. He hadn't wanted to make any assumptions, though he had assigned her the dessert station, so they'd be the last two in the kitchen. He'd been surprised when she'd brushed her lips against his. But not upset.

She'd come to his house on Sunday for their cooking adventures. He didn't mind. And she'd asked him to go to the VIP Pool grand opening that morning with her.

Ah, the slacks. No wonder she was wearing them, and Teagan panicked over his choice of jeans and his regular black kitchen shoes. And he couldn't even remember what he'd put on underneath his chef's jacket.

The grand opening was at noon, and he told himself he'd have time to change as he heard a rush of noise fill the restaurant just beyond the kitchen. He drew in a deep breath and focused, which meant he had to push Gwen and her sexy slacks out of his mind so he could make fried potatoes and peach waffles.

YOU'RE LATE. GWEN'S TEXT DIDN'T MAKE TRAFFIC MOVE ANY faster, and Teagan realized he shouldn't have left the inn to go home and change. He simply hadn't anticipated so many people piling into The Heartwood Inn for a pool grand opening.

It was a swimming pool, for crying out loud. The inn boasted seven of them on its sprawling grounds, but apparently, this new indoor one was a Big Deal.

I'm five minutes out, he typed back to her. The app on his phone said that, at least, and then he'd park and sprint up to the second floor.

It starts in five minutes, she said.

Can't you get them to hold it? he asked. Surely all these people are coming to it.

Is there a lot of traffic?

Where else did she think he was? Chilling on the beach? He suppressed a sigh and told himself not to get annoyed. *I'm pretty sure I see the mayor's car a few in front of me*, he rapidly typed. *Surely he's coming to this grand opening.*

Teagan knew he was, because Gwen's sister, Celeste, had decided to name the pool after the mayor's wife. Apparently, she was a Carter's Cove native, and she'd once been a swimming champion.

Whatever. Teagan didn't care. What he cared about was being at Gwen's side when she needed him there.

Let me check with Celeste.

The two sisters lived together, and Teagan knew Gwen was very close to her sister. He wondered what Gwen had said about him. What it would say when he showed up at her side, his hand linked with hers.

The cars inched forward, and if he could just get another hundred feet, he could turn left into the employee parking lot while everyone else had to stay to the right. He edged that way, moving feet at a time until he could almost make the turn.

Frustration built with impatience, and he really wanted to lay on the horn and get the car in front of him to just pull up a little bit more. He had to have a couple more feet.

He gripped the wheel as his phone bleeped out the notification that he had a new message. *You have until the mayor gets here.*

And his car wasn't up to the hotel yet.

Teagan finally got to make his turn, and he parked as close to the kitchen entrance as he could. Inside, he dashed past Gwen's office and toward the front lobby. A group of people waited at the elevator, so Teagan opened the door for the stairs and kept on moving. It was only one flight, and he arrived on the second floor to the scent of flowers and chlorine, the two smells at odds with one another.

A decent crowd had gathered here too, and the elevator chimed and opened to let off even more.

He spied the Heartwoods standing at the head of the pool, where a podium and microphone had been set up. Teagan froze, watching Gwen as she scanned the crowd for him. She looked nervous, and he felt all of those electric zips and swoops in his stomach as he realized he was going to be meeting all of the Heartwoods.

Right now.

All five sisters stood there, all of them with men beside them—except Gwen. Her parents stood the closest to the podium, and Gwen's elderly grandmother had her arm linked through Gwen's.

In that moment, Teagan could see himself in the hole in that family. He blinked, his eyes closing so slowly and then opening again. In that single space of time, he saw himself on Gwen's other side, smiling out at everyone who'd come to see this new indoor pool.

And he couldn't move.

Was this what he wanted?

You want Gwen, he told himself. His eyes moved down the line, and he caught sight of Chet, Olympia's boyfriend. The man had worked beachside service for the surfing championship several weeks ago, and Teagan liked him.

Celeste often texted him her food orders, and he'd shake his head and make sure she got what she wanted in record time. Gage, Sheryl's boyfriend, was their new head baker, and he'd been doing a bang-up job with the bakery portion of the dining services at the inn. He knew Alissa from her years as the head baker in the kitchens. In fact, it had been Alissa who'd hired him.

Teagan had friends over there, and he managed to take the first step toward going to Gwen's side. She seemed to catch sight of him in the very next moment, and Teagan lifted his hand to acknowledge that he was finally there.

He pressed through the crowd and stepped into that hole in her family, and it...fit.

"Hey," she said, reaching over to take his hand in hers. "It must be nuts out there."

"Completely," he said, glancing at Gage, who had his eyebrows raised. He nodded at the man and leaned down so he could whisper in Gwen's ear without being overheard. "Am I meeting the whole family today?"

"Um, probably," she whispered back.

"And I'm...." He wasn't sure how to finish that sentence. In fact, he wanted *Gwen* to finish it.

"You're with me," she said as her father finally stepped over to the microphone and adjusted it.

Teagan squeezed her hand, unsure of what *you're with me* meant. Boyfriend? Kitchen support? What was he to her?

She kisses you, he told himself. You're her boyfriend.

And he couldn't help the smile that slid onto his face with that label. Better to get the goofy grinning done now, so he didn't do it when she introduced him that way to her father.

9

Gwen's muscles clenched, and she couldn't seem to get them to relax. Her father spoke into the microphone, but she barely heard a word he said. She laughed when everyone else did, and she kept her Heartwood smile on her face.

After the morning meeting in the kitchen, she'd hurried home so Celeste could curl her hair. The wave would be gone in a couple of hours, but it would serve its purpose for the pictures that would be taken once the mayor's wife said a few words.

She wore too much makeup, and she wondered what Teagan thought of it. His presence behind her felt solid, strong, and warm, and she kept glancing at Celeste. But her sister and best friend kept her eyes glued to the podium as if the Queen of England herself was thanking the family for the honor of having a swimming pool named after them.

And it wasn't even a swimming pool anyone could use. Only platinum and diamond-level guests who got the right keycard upon check-in.

After Amanda George finished, and after the applause died down, Olympia stepped up to the microphone. She looked poised and relaxed, and Gwen marveled at her oldest sister. She was professional and polished and personable all at the same time, and Gwen couldn't even imagine the load Olympia carried.

She was taking some time off in October to go meet Chet's family, as his sister had a party planned, and Gwen's father's words about taking time off when she needed it echoed through her mind.

Take the time you need.

The kitchen will be fine without you.

"We now dedicate this pool to the life and love of swimming exhibited by Amanda George, and to all The Heartwood Inn guests who will enjoy it." Olympia started clapping, and Gwen joined in. That was also her cue to get up to the podium with everyone else, and she linked her hand with Teagan's to bring him along.

This photo would be printed in the local newspapers. Online. And as a photograph that would hang in the inn for a long time. Her heart pinched at the very idea of having to walk by it to get to Celeste's office and seeing Teagan beside her. What if they broke up?

Regret lanced through her. Perhaps she shouldn't have invited him. But none of her sisters had said a word about it, and they didn't usually hold back.

Cameras clicked and chatter broke out. Celeste stepped to the mic and said, "Refreshments are right around the corner in our Dolphin Room. Please, let's move in that direction." She too was made to be in front of people, and Gwen's emotions spiraled all over the place.

She moved, keeping Teagan's hand securely in hers. "Is this your new boyfriend, Gwen?" Shawn asked, and Gwen nearly fell down.

"Yes," she said, glad he'd said the B-word. "Teagan Hatch. This is Alissa's boyfriend, Shawn Newman." The two men shook hands, and Alissa smiled at Teagan and started telling Shawn how she'd worked with him in the kitchen there at the inn.

"Ah, got it," Shawn said, nodding. "I know who you are now. How long have you and Gwen been dating?"

"Shawn," Alissa said. "Come check on the smoked salmon with me." She linked her arm through his and drew him away from Gwen and Teagan.

"What?" Gwen heard him ask. "It's a normal question." Her sister leaned her head closer to Shawn and spoke, and Gwen sent a mental note of gratitude toward Alissa.

"Sorry," she said.

"It's fine," Teagan said. "I could've answered the question."

"Yeah? What would you have said?"

"Not long," he said with a smile. "It's true, right?" He squeezed her hand, and Gwen supposed it was true. They'd only gone out for a few weeks before he'd broken up with her last time, so "not long" fit for how long they'd been dating.

Now, seeing each other...that was a different story. She'd been "seeing" Teagan at work for years. Crushing on him for much of that. Finally getting up her courage to let him know she was interested had been very difficult, but she thought the result could be fantastic.

Then he'd broken her heart.

And he was slowly repairing it too.

"Hey," Gage said. "Good to see you two here together." He smiled at them and picked up a glass of punch. Celeste had gone all out for the dedication, and Gwen looked at the trays of finger foods she and her catering team had made the day before. She usually didn't mind eating the food she'd made, but today, the sight of the canapes and tiny sandwiches turned her stomach sour.

"Is this the new boyfriend?" her father asked, and Gwen turned toward him. She really hadn't thought through her invitation for Teagan to accompany her to this dedication.

"Yes, Dad," she said. "This is Teagan Hatch. He's the head chef here at the inn. Teagan, my father, Henry."

"So nice to meet you, sir," he said. "I mean, officially. I've met you before, of course."

Her dad smiled at Teagan. "Right. Bea probably hired you, right?"

"Actually, Alissa hired me," he said, glancing at Gwen. She'd been working in the kitchen as a chef when Teagan had been hired at the inn five years ago. She'd been a year out of culinary school, thinking she was the most amazing person to ever pick up a knife, when he walked in and changed how she viewed food. And cooking. And how a kitchen should run.

He was almost a decade older than her, with much more experience under his belt, and she'd soaked in everything she could. Her crush had probably started then, though it was definitely on a professional level for a while.

She realized her father and Teagan were talking and laughing, and Gwen brought herself back to the conversation. "I never say no to a homecooked meal," her father said.

"Mom cooks," Gwen said just as her mother arrived.

"Oh, only a couple nights a week," she said. "What are we talking about?"

"Teagan's going to come cook for us," her dad said, beaming at Teagan.

Gwen and her mother said, "He is?" at the same time.

"Sure," he said easily.

"How are you going to do that when you work every night at Redfin?" Gwen asked. She searched his face, so she saw the flash of anger as it blinked through his eyes. It was like a bolt of lightning. There one second and gone the next.

"Teagan," Olympia said, joining the crowd. She looked at Gwen and back to Teagan. "You two are back together?"

"Yes," Teagan said at the same time Gwen said, "Kind of."

"Kind of?" Olympia and Teagan said together, and everything spiraled out of control. Gwen's thoughts spun, and she had no idea what to say. Or why she'd said that.

Her dad put his hand on Olympia's shoulder and said, "Maybe we should let them figure it out," and he started to move away.

Olympia stayed, looking from Gwen to Teagan and back. She leaned in and hugged Gwen, saying, "You never really got along all that well, did you?" She pulled away and walked away, her fingers tapping on her phone. O was exceptionally skilled at getting the word out to people, and Celeste and Sheryl kept their distance.

"Can we talk?" Teagan asked while Olympia's words reverberated in Gwen's brain.

Fear struck Gwen right behind her pulse. "I don't know why I said that," she said. "Of course we're together again."

"Are we?" His eyebrows went up as if he was challenging her. "What did your sister say?" She'd seen this hard look on his face in the kitchen too, and it annoyed her as much then as it did now.

"I'm sorry," she said, because she *had* been the one to

say something she shouldn't. "Yes, we're together. I introduced you as my boyfriend."

"Actually," Teagan said slowly. "I don't think you ever said it."

"I said yes when my dad said it," Gwen said, desperate to make this right.

Teagan leaned closer, examining her. "What's going on in there, Gwenny?"

Tears gathered in her eyes, and she had no idea why. "I don't know. Maybe this...maybe I shouldn't have invited you to this when the whole family was here. Maybe we're still a little new at this, and maybe...." She shrugged, glad her tears hadn't leaked out. "I don't know."

"New at this," he repeated, not unkindly. Teagan could be blunt and brusque, especially in the kitchen. But he was never unkind. Even when there was a conflict with another chef, he got through the meal service, and then talked it out with the person.

She didn't know what to say, and she just wanted to leave this reception. She glanced around, wondering if there were enough Heartwoods here that she could. Deciding there were, she turned and headed for the exit, glad when Teagan came with her.

"Just to be clear," he said. "I also didn't appreciate you challenging my ability to make a meal for your parents, right in front of them."

Misery combined with Gwen's guilt, and she looked at the ground. "I didn't mean to do that."

He slipped his hand in hers. “I know you didn’t.” He nudged her toward a corner and they turned it together. He stepped in front of her, making her stop and look up at him. “You want to be back together with me, don’t you?”

“Absolutely, I do,” she said, hoping he could hear the absolute truth in those words. “I don’t know. I got nervous, and I wasn’t thinking, and my sister is wrong. We get along fine.”

His eyebrows went up again, this time laced with surprise. “She said we didn’t?”

“Something like that,” Gwen mumbled.

Teagan drew in a deep breath. “I think the reason we didn’t work out last time was because of me, Gwen. All me. I didn’t allow myself to open up to you and really talk to you. Tell you things you needed to know.” He took both of her hands in his. “But I did that this time. Or I’m willing to do that. And I think we get along great. Cooking with you, talking to you, working with you, it’s all fun for me.”

“For me too,” she said.

“Then forget about what Olympia said, and tell me I’m your boyfriend.”

Gwen grinned at him and said, “You’re my boyfriend.”

He smiled back, his hands coming up to cradle her face. “I’m going to kiss my girlfriend now.” And he did, and Gwen’s anxiety decreased. Her nerves quieted. And she felt safe in the arms of this man who clearly liked her.

“So no kind of,” she whispered when he pulled away.

"No kind of, Gwenny," he said. "We're either both in this, or we're not."

"I can live with that." She tipped up on her toes and kissed him again, glad he could forgive her when she said two stupid words.

GWEN'S HEART TREMBLED AS SHE MADE HER WAY DOWN THE hall in the administrative wing of the hotel. Olympia would surely be back in her office by now. That, or she'd taken the afternoon off to spend time with Chet.

Her oldest sister had been loosening up the last couple of months or so. She used to walk through the kitchen each morning with Gwen, and she hadn't done so for a few days now.

Gwen knocked on her sister's office door and then opened it.

"Heya, sissy," Olympia said, turning from the coffee maker on the counter. "I'm so sorry about what I said about Teagan."

Gwen entered the office and closed the door, grateful for the quick apology. "I know he asked you out once, and you weren't interested."

"But that doesn't mean you shouldn't go out with him if you like him." She stirred her coffee and sat down at her desk. "He's a great guy. Just not my type."

"Who's not your type?"

Gwen swung around to see Olympia's boyfriend, Chet, entering the office. "Hey, Gwen," he said with a smile. He moved over to O and leaned down to kiss her. "I hope you weren't talking about me. I feel awkward now."

She laughed, and Gwen smiled as she sat in the comfy chair across from her sister. "We were talking about Gwen's boyfriend," she said. "Do either of you want coffee?"

"None for me," Gwen said, and Chet stepped over to the maker and started making himself a cup.

"Nice guy," Chet said. "Very detailed at what he does. Skilled in the kitchen."

Gwen blinked at Chet. Had Olympia given him a script?

"Chet consults for us," Olympia said. "He knows Teagan well enough."

Chet turned back to the women and lifted his mug to his lips. "Word on the street is that Gwen knows Teagan really well."

"What does that mean?" Gwen asked, suddenly horrified.

Chet chuckled. "You two are dating, right?"

"Yes," Gwen said. "And we get along fine." She glared at her sister.

"I shouldn't have said that."

"You told her they don't get along?" Chet asked.

"I said it *seemed* like they didn't get along," O said, glancing at her boyfriend. "It wasn't my place."

"Yeah, because we shouldn't talk," Chet said.

Olympia giggled and leaned back in her chair, must more at-ease than Gwen had ever seen her. "I suppose you're right."

"You guys didn't get along?" she asked.

"Oh, we bicker like an old married couple," Chet said. "Everything doesn't have to be perfect in a relationship. You just have to be committed to making it work, and you have to forgive."

Gwen nodded, because she thought that was probably true. "Opposites attract and all that," she said.

"Exactly," Olympia said. "So forget I said anything. You obviously like Teagan, and he seems *quite* enamored with you." Her eyes sparkled with mischief. "Now, do you have anything business related? It's my break, and I want to kiss my boyfriend." She grinned at Gwen, who stood quickly.

"Nothing business related. I just wanted...talk to you later." She got out of the office before the kissing started, because she did not need to see that. Hope filled her steps as she went back to the kitchen. Hope for her and Teagan. And hope that she could catch a nap on the couch in her office.

10

Almost a week later, Teagan wiped his hands on his towel and said, "I'll be back in a minute." They were twenty minutes away from finishing breakfast service, and there were no orders.

"Yep," Gordon said, wiping the counter.

Gwen had asked him to come see her when he had a minute, and he had about five right now. He walked over to her open office door and knocked as he said, "You wanted to see me?"

She looked up from the long piece of paper she taped together every week to make their schedule. Pure exhaustion lived in her expression, and Teagan's idea to take her to lunch withered instantly. She needed to go home and take a nap—not that he'd ever tell her that.

"Come in," she said. "And close the door behind you."

Teagan did as she said, his pulse bouncing in anticipation of what this little meeting would be. She had two straight-backed chairs in front of the desk, and he sat in one of them.

"Look at this, would you?" she turned the complex schedule toward him. "I want to make sure everything is covered."

"Covered for what?" he asked. She'd never asked for his input in making the schedule. Or reviewing it. Nothing.

"I'm taking a trip," she said. "I need a vacation."

Teagan looked up from the spreadsheet, surprised. "A vacation?"

She giggled and shook her head. "You say that like you don't know what one is."

"Well, I mean, I've heard of them." He grinned at her. "Good for you. Where are you going?"

"I haven't decided yet," she said. "It's not until next weekend, and I want to make sure everything is set here before I go."

"How long will you be gone?" He peered at the chart again, looking through room service assignments, catering jobs, the bakery, and Redfin.

"Ten days," she said.

He almost always found his name on the catering events, the breakfast orders for the bakery, and Redfin in the evenings. In fact, that was always where he worked.

But his name wasn't on this schedule at all. His eyebrows drew down, and he started looking more earnestly. "I'm sure I'll be able to help...." His voice faded as he continued to study the paper in front of him.

"You're not going to be here to help," she said, and Teagan lifted his eyes to hers. "At least, I hope not."

"You hope not?"

"You're really cute when you're confused." She gave him a coy smile, but Teagan could see the brimming fear in her eyes.

He sat back, ready to wait for her to clue him in. He folded his arms and cocked his eyebrows at her when she remained silent.

Her throat moved as she swallowed once, and then twice. Her nerves filled the whole office. "I'm hoping you'll come to Whistlestop Shores. With me. For ten days."

Surprise hit him like an explosion, suddenly there one moment when it hadn't been before. His mind whirred, and a strangled noise came from his throat, because he felt like he should say something, but he didn't know what.

"Take some time to think about it," Gwen said, her fun, flirty smiles gone. "I already have a couple of things planned. Tickets and such."

"For me?" he asked.

She shrugged, which meant yes.

"Accommodations?" he asked. They could be very hard to get on Whistlestop, as if there was any island as busy as Carter's Cove, it was Whistlestop Shores.

"Secured," she said.

Teagan drew in a breath and employed his bravery too. "Okay, I need to know specifics about that one," he said. "Like, you have one room for us to share? Or two, and we'll spend the day together but sleep separately?"

"I have a phone call out," she said. "I'm waiting to book the room or rooms until I know how many guests there will be." She slid the schedule back in front of her. "But if you wanted to come, there would be two rooms. I like you, but I don't think we're ready for...that."

Relief hit Teagan, because he agreed wholeheartedly. Whatever her "that" was, Teagan agreed. He had some "that's" of his own.

"Can I get back to you?"

"Of course." She sounded cool and professional, and Teagan hated that he couldn't just say yes. This invitation simply felt...sudden, and he'd just barely figured out how to tell Gwen about his daughter. They'd only been back together for ten days, and now she wanted to take a trip together that would last that long.

"I do need to post this by tomorrow evening," she said. "If you'd let me know by then."

"I can do that," Teagan said, standing up. "I better go see what Gordon needs." But he knew Gordon didn't need anything. He still felt like he was escaping from Gwen's office, only to find the kitchen nearly clean and Gordon hangin up his apron for the day.

"Done?" he asked his friend.

"Yep. Margo said they cut off orders for hot food." Gordon smiled at him. "What were you doing in there?"

"Uh." Teagan looked over his shoulder. "You know I'm seeing Gwen, right?"

"The whole kitchen knows."

Teagan didn't know what that meant. He and Gwen hadn't kept their relationship a secret, and she didn't favor him. He'd earned the head chef position before she'd even taken over control of the dining services at the inn.

"So she calls you in there so you can kiss her?" Gordon grinned like he had the entire universe figured out.

"I wish." Teagan scoffed. "What are you doing right now? I need to ask you a question." And call his mother. His sister. His daughter. Maybe with four other opinions, he'd be able to come up with the right answer to Gwen's invitation.

"Let's go get lunch," Gordon said, and he swiped his keys from the peg by the metal door that led out to the parking lot.

Teagan felt out of sorts as he followed Gordon down the coast a bit, the group of food stands on the beach finally coming into view. They each went to the one they wanted and met at a picnic table in full sun.

"So what's up?" Gordon asked, biting into his breakfast crepe. Teagan had opted for a box of mini doughnuts and a cappuccino.

"She asked me to go on a trip with her," he said. "To Whistlestop Shores."

"Oh, okay, so we're far along in our relationship." Gordon's eyes widened, and Teagan felt validated in his concerns just from that simple action.

"Not really," Teagan said. "That's the thing. We dated for a few weeks about six months ago. And I messed up and did something stupid. Then I fixed it, and we've been seeing each other for just over a week now."

"One room or two?"

"Two."

"Oh, so she wants a vacation, and she wants some company." Gordon shrugged and folded over his crepe. "That's different, I think."

"Is it?"

"I don't know," Gordon said. "Once, a woman I went out with broke up with me after three dates because I ordered wrong at a restaurant." He took another bite of his food, and Teagan lifted a chocolate mini doughnut out of the box.

"How do you order wrong at a restaurant?" Teagan asked, and Gordon started laughing. Teagan joined in, because he seriously didn't understand women sometimes.

"I have no idea," Gordon said between chuckles. "My best advice—and I have no idea what I'm talking about—is to go with your gut. You like Gwen, obviously. Do you *want* to take a trip with her?"

Teagan didn't answer, because he didn't know what his gut was saying. He was supremely glad he hadn't asked a female for advice about this first, and he nixed the idea to call the women in his life and ask them.

He and Gordon finished their food and talked about the upcoming football season as easily as if they went to breakfast after work every week. They didn't, but their friendship was easy, even with time going by in between the things they did do.

As he drove back to his apartment, he realized his relationship with Gwen was the same way. They'd seemingly picked up right where they'd left off, even though there had been six painful, long, trying months in between the time he'd walked her to her door and broken up with her, and the day he'd showed up to take her to lunch and confess a few things about his past.

And his gut knew—he wanted to go on vacation with her. He grabbed his phone and typed out a message. *I'd love to go to Whistlestop Shores with you. Want me to play tour guide, or is that not on the agenda?*

Why else do you think I asked you? ;)

Teagan chuckled at Gwen's response and went out onto the balcony that overlooked the water on the eastern side of the island. He looked north, as if he'd be able to see his home island from here. He couldn't, but he knew he'd need to call his mother and sister and let them know he was coming—and bringing a woman—home.

He had a fine relationship with his sister, but his relationship with his mother had been up and down over the years. He'd thought that was what he wanted. He had people he talked to. An amazing job he'd always wanted. Money. A great apartment.

He didn't need to go home for Thanksgiving or Christmas, and he was fine with sending a birthday cards to his loved ones when the occasion required it.

But he couldn't go to Whistlestop Shores without even telling them. He might be able to get away with just having one nice dinner with them and calling it good, but he wouldn't know until he called.

So he picked up his phone and dialed his mother, hoping his day wasn't about to get astronomically worse.

"Teagan," his mother said, and he imagined her sitting on her back deck, a bowl of trail mix beside her. She loved the stuff, and she loved watching people, and she loved evening walks.

"Hello, Mother," he said, drawing on his Southern manners and upbringing. "How are you?"

"Just fine, dear. What has you calling?"

"I'm coming back to the Shores for a bit," he said, wishing she wasn't quite so formal with him. But she always had been, even when he was a child. "Wondered if you and the family might want to get together for dinner." He breathed in deeply, sure Tilly would want to see him. She had twin ten-year-old girls, and Teagan sent them money on their birthday.

"Why, I'm sure we would," she said. "When are you coming?"

He pressed his eyes closed and took another deep

breath. "I'll have to check with my girlfriend on that one, Mom, but not until next weekend. Sometime after that."

"Girlfriend?"

Teagan smiled, because he did like calling Gwen that, whether she was present or not. "That's right, Mom. Her name is Gwen."

"This isn't going to end like the last one, is it?" she asked, and all of the reasons Teagan just sent cards on holidays came rushing back.

"The last one was twenty years ago, Mother," he said with maybe a little more bite than he intended. "People change, you know."

Of course, she hadn't, so she probably thought he was that same irresponsible, hot-headed nineteen-year-old that had gotten married on a whim.

"It's been so long since you came home," his mom said next, as if Teagan hadn't spoken at all.

"I know," he said. "I'll call Tilly and set everything up, okay?"

"Yes," his mother said. "Call Tilly. She'll know what to do."

Teagan said his formal goodbyes and got off the phone quickly. "You should've known to call Tilly first," he muttered to himself, because now he had one more phone call to make. And for a man who hated to make phone calls, he'd already reached his limit with the last one.

So he decided to start with a text instead. *Hey, Tilly.*

Coming to the Shores next weekend with my girlfriend. What do you think of dinner with everyone?

His thoughts felt laced with poison, and he wondered if he could convince Gwen to take their vacation somewhere else.

Nope, he told himself. *You're not running from this.* He'd promised himself he wouldn't do that again, and he was going to stick with that. He'd have to introduce Gwen to his family sooner or later.

"Might as well be sooner," he said as his phone chimed with Tilly's response. Even if he was dreading the visit.

Sure, his sister had said. *Tell me about this girlfriend.... She must be something if you're willing to bring her to the Shores.*

11

Gwen looked up from the pile of clothes on her bed when her sister walked into the room. "Packing?" Celeste said, leaning over to remove her high heels.

"Yep." Gwen popped the P on the word, telling herself not to call Teagan and back out. Not that she'd actually call. Oh, no. She'd text. Then there wouldn't be any awkward silences while she tried to figure out why she was so dang nervous.

"You're freaking out," Celeste said, sweeping her shoes into the hallway behind her.

"What was the first clue?" Gwen asked, her panic sending shudders through her muscles.

"Well, you have tons of clothes here," Celeste said. "And you always know exactly what to wear." She shrugged and smiled. "And besides, it's still super warm outside, and you're going to another island, with your boyfriend, who is *super hot*. You should only have Daisy dukes and tanks and bikini tops as options."

"I'm too old for Daisy dukes."

"No, you are not," Celeste said. "You just turned thirty, and I've seen way older women wear them."

"Runners," Gwen said, thinking of the extra weight she carried. It came from all the tasting in the kitchen she had to do. At least that was what she'd told herself when she hadn't been able to shimmy into her favorite pair of skinny jeans last Valentine's Day.

"The second clue was that I got home five minutes ago with dinner, and you didn't come out to the kitchen." Celeste picked up a stack of blouses and took them back to Gwen's dresser. "You're the fashion expert, sis, but seriously. No."

Gwen sat down on the bed in the now-empty spot, a sigh leaking from her lips. "I'm nervous."

"Good," Celeste said. "It's a good thing to be nervous." She returned to the bed and sat down beside Gwen, nudging over a pile of bathing suits to do it. "What are you nervous about, specifically? You have two rooms, right?"

"Yes," Gwen said. "And they connect. Jamey was very accommodating, and we're on a high floor, with beach views."

"And Teagan knows that you're not going to sleep with him."

"Right. We've talked about the accommodations. He says he's happy about the arrangements." There had been a lot of talking over the past ten days in preparation for the next ten days.

"So what are you nervous about? You get to spend time with him on a magical island, eat great food, and kiss him good-night before you get your alone time overlooking the beach."

"You make it sound so effortless." Gwen looked at Celeste. "What if I don't like being with him for twelve hours a day? For ten days."

"Then tell him that. You say, 'hey, I want to do something on my own tomorrow. Let's meet up for dinner, okay?' and what's he going to do? Say no?" Celeste reached over and tucked Gwen's hair behind her ear, and Gwen could not imagine living in this house without her sister.

But Celeste had a serious boyfriend who was also a decade older than her, and Gwen would be shocked if she wasn't the first to get engaged. All of the sisters had boyfriends now, but Gwen knew Olympia would come back from her trip to meet Chet's family with a diamond too.

Alissa and Shawn were taking things a little slower. A little more casual. But they seemed very happy to be together, as did Gage and Sheryl.

"Do people do that?" Gwen asked. "Go on vacation together and then spend time apart?"

"Absolutely they do," Celeste said. "Otherwise, there would be more deaths on vacation." She grinned and giggled, and some of Gwen's nervous energy evaporated. "Now come on," her sister said. "I stopped for pizza like you said, and you like everything so hot."

"I like hot food to be hot," Gwen said, abandoning her clothing choices and following Celeste out of the room and down the hall to the kitchen. Celeste opened the pizza box to reveal a cheesy pepperoni pizza, and love swelled in her heart. "You don't even like pepperoni pizza."

"But you do, and I knew you'd be nervous." Celeste opened a box of breadsticks, her eyes crinkling with happiness. "I got what I wanted."

"Ooh, pure carbs," Gwen said, reaching for a slice of pizza. No plate required, which was sometimes a relief after having to make every plate so beautiful for the guests at The Heartwood Inn. "Is Brad coming over tonight?"

"Yes, but he's working on the outdoor wedding hall for a while." Celeste dipped her breadstick in the marinara sauce and took a bite. A groan came from her mouth, and her eyes rolled back in her head. It really was a miracle what bread and garlic and marinara sauce could do for a woman.

Gwen took a bite of her cheesy pizza, her reaction quite similar to Celeste's. Maybe this trip would be okay. Maybe she and Teagan really would have ten magical days where they fell in love and planned a future together.

Gwen tried to pull her head out of the clouds. After all, she'd been up in the stratosphere when it came to

Teagan before, and she didn't need to make that mistake again. He'd been stitching her heart back together minute by minute, event by event, conversation by conversation, but Gwen knew she wasn't whole yet.

She and Celeste had finished eating and had cleaned up when someone knocked on the front door. She said, "Come on, Joey," but the dog ran for the door, barking his fool head off. Midnight followed, her claws skidding on the floor as she added her higher voice to the fray.

"Quiet," Celeste admonished from where she'd curled into herself on the couch. "It's just Brad." She got up to answer the door, and Gwen wanted to retreat to the screened-in back porch. She'd take the dogs with her, and Celeste and Brad could have the house to themselves.

"She never used to bark until you took Joey," Gwen said, walking over to the black poodle and scooping her up. "And why didn't he just come in?" Brad always walked in after knocking.

Gwen opened the door, saying, "You can just come in —oh." Teagan stood on the front step, and he reached up and ran his hand through that gorgeous flop of hair. "Teagan."

"Come on, girl." Celeste appeared at her side and took the little dog from Gwen. "You guys go on out back."

But Gwen didn't move. "What are you doing here?" she asked.

"I called a couple of times," he said, smiling at her. "I was in the neighborhood, and I'm hungry, and I thought maybe you and I could grab some dinner we don't have to cook."

"I've—"

"Hey," Brad said as he came up the steps. He clapped Teagan on the back. "I didn't get to meet you at the grand opening. I'm Bradley Keith."

"Yeah, of course," Teagan said. "The football star."

"He's my sister's boyfriend," Gwen said. "She took the dogs out back. Can't you hear Joey barking?"

"Hey, at least he stopped chewing her shoes."

"Well, for a day," Gwen said as Brad pushed through Teagan and Gwen and entered the house. He walked toward the back door like he owned the place, and Gwen watched him go before turning back to her own boyfriend.

"Dinner would be great," she said, though she'd eaten two pieces of pizza only twenty minutes ago.

"Before we go, I just have to say something," he said. "I'm nervous about tomorrow." He slicked his hands down the front of his jeans. "There. That's it. I thought if I saw you I'd be less nervous."

Gwen gave him a smile. "I'm scared out of my mind."

He started laughing, and Gwen joined in. She kept giggling as she bent to put on her shoes. "But you were right. I'm less nervous now that I'm face-to-face with you."

Teagan reached for her hand, and she pulled the front door closed behind her. "Why do you think we're nervous?"

"I'm not sure," Gwen said. "We see each other every day. Morning and night."

"But I still get to go home at night," he said. "Not that I don't want you home with me. I mean—I'm going to stop talking now."

"I know what you mean," Gwen said. "I'm an introvert too, though I wouldn't classify you as one."

"No?" he asked. "I'm more of a hermit, I guess."

Gwen burst out laughing. "That's not what I meant. You run a kitchen like a pro. Guiding plenty of people."

"But I don't actually hang out with them." He cocked an eyebrow at her. "I don't like people."

"Yes, you do," she said, scoffing.

"I tolerate most people. I like you, though." He opened her door for her, and Gwen slid into the passenger seat. She thought about what he'd said while he circled the car and got behind the wheel.

"We don't have to go to Whistlestop Shores," she said. "There's still quite a lot of people there."

"Oh, we have to go," he said. "We're having dinner with my mother and my sister's family tomorrow night."

"So they confirmed," Gwen said, a new tremor in her stomach.

"A couple of hours ago," he said. "Leave it to Tilly to wait until the last moment. I guess her husband had something he had to work out."

"At least it's the first night, right?" Gwen asked. She hadn't met his family yet, but Teagan had said they were hard to be around, thus why he didn't go visit though Whistlestop Shores was only three hours up the coast.

"Tilly's fine," he said. "I don't know her husband well, but he's usually fine too. It's just my mother."

"Beverly, right?"

"That's right," Teagan said. "What are we feeling like tonight? Pizza?"

"I actually ate pizza already," she said, drawing his attention.

"What? When?"

"Half an hour ago," she said with a smile. "But I wanted to go out with you." She'd never been so open and honest with a man as she was with Teagan.

He chuckled and shook his head. "So sushi then. You don't like it, and I do, and this feels like the right time for us to venture down that road."

"They'll have avocado rolls," Gwen said. "And I like those."

"And tempura," he said. "And that's one of my favorite foods."

"Is tempura a food group?" she teased.

"Totally," he said. "And I want it right now." He took a right, and they pulled into the Japanese restaurant a moment later.

"I like some sushi," she said, looking up at the sign. "And this is a great place, I've heard."

"So you're going to try it?"

"I'm doing all kinds of new things lately," she said.

"Taking vacations, eating dinner twice in one night, and saying all kinds of things I never would've before."

"And eating sushi," he said, grinning at her.

They met at the front of the car, and Gwen put her hand on his arm. "So you know, you're the one who inspires me to say what I'm really feeling."

He simply looked at her. "Why?"

"Because you showed up for lunch when we got back together and told me things you didn't want to. Sometimes we just have to say what we're thinking and feeling, but I've never really done that." Everything inside her quaked just a little bit. "At least not with a man."

Teagan's slow smile made her heart beat rapidly for a different reason, and he leaned down and touched his lips to hers in the sweetest kiss.

And Gwen wondered why she'd been so nervous.

12

Teagan pulled up to Gwen's house again the next morning much later than he was used to seeing her. The sun was well up into the sky, and Teagan hadn't woken up while everyone else still slumbered.

The front door opened before he'd taken two steps, and Gwen came out with her bag. "I'm coming," he called to her so she didn't try to heave it down the steps herself.

She flashed him a quick smile and then ducked back into the house, saying something to the dogs there. Teagan went up the steps and took her bag back to the trunk of his car. He looked at hers next to his, and something peaceful moved through him.

He'd hardly been able to sleep last night in anticipation of this trip, but now more excitement than anxiety filled him. Back at the front door, he found Gwen feeding the dogs as she talked to her sister.

"...going to be great," Celeste said. "Don't think too much. Enjoy your time off with that handsome man."

Gwen said something Teagan couldn't quite catch, and the sisters laughed. He entered the house then, because he didn't want to eavesdrop on his girlfriend and hear something he didn't want to hear.

"Ready?" he asked.

"Just about," Gwen said, twisting toward him. "I need that beach bag on the couch too. You can take that out. I just need to find my phone...." She patted all of her pockets while Teagan collected her bag and turned to leave again.

"Joey," Celeste called, but the dog caught up to him and preceded him out the front door.

"Stay here," he told the dog, who trotted down the steps and onto the front lawn. "Joey, stay."

The dog sniffed around, clearly not going to run off, and Teagan put the beach bag in the trunk too. Gwen had gotten them rooms at a very nice hotel—one of the nicest on the Shores—and Teagan couldn't wait to see how many swimming suits she'd packed.

"Come on, boy," he said to the dog, and they went back up the steps together. He nearly ran into Gwen coming out, and they laughed as he grabbed onto her so they wouldn't fall.

"Bye, Celeste," Gwen said over her shoulder, and Teagan stepped back so they could walk to the car together.

A blast of nerves hit him as soon as everything was in, all the doors were closed, and he sat behind the steering wheel. He drew in a deep breath. "All right," he said, exhaling hard. "We're really doing this?"

"Yes," Gwen said, nodding to the windshield. "I actually slept until eight-thirty this morning," she said. "It was amazing." She looked at him with a new light in her eyes, and Teagan had the sudden impression that Vacation Gwen was going to be very different than Kitchen Gwen.

And he couldn't wait to find out what Whistlestop Shores had in store for them.

TEAGAN STOOD AT THE WINDOW AND WATCHED THE WAVES roll in. The view from his room was spectacular, and whatever connections Gwen had here was on the island were serious. He'd been ready to hit the beach for ten minutes, but Gwen said she'd knock on the door connecting their rooms when she was ready.

That sound came in the next moment, and Teagan turned toward the door at the same time it opened. Gwen walked through, and he froze, unable to move. She wore a floral-patterned bikini top that left his throat dry and his lungs breathless. Paired with that, she had a pair of extremely short denim shorts on, the ends fraying while they barely covered any leg.

"Wow," she said, and he realized she was raking her

eyes down his body too. He suddenly felt self-conscious standing there in his swimming trunks and nothing else.

"Yeah, no kidding," he said, grabbing his towel and holding it in front of his body. He cleared his throat, trying to remember how to think, how to walk, how to act normal.

"No kidding?" Gwen cocked her head as if she didn't know what he meant. His feet had done a lot of walking, and they managed to move over to her.

"Yeah, no kidding," he murmured. "Wow times two. Double-wow." He let his fingers trail down her bare arm, never removing his eyes from hers. In the next moment, he kissed her, the union of their mouths a little rougher than it ever had been in the past.

His hands met bare skin on her back, and Teagan had never been happier to come to the beach. Gwen matched him stroke for stroke, her hands sliding over his shoulders and up into his hair.

He pulled away breathing heavily, and fell back a step. Then two. "Sorry." He'd dropped his towel during the exchange, and he bent to pick it up.

"I can put that in my bag," she said, taking it from him. Her voice sounded as ragged as he felt. "Should we go?"

"Yes, let's go." He couldn't stay in this room with her for very much longer. They went downstairs and on down to the beach, where she found a spot of sand and laid out their towels. She sighed as she sat down and stretched those impossibly long legs in front of her.

"Vacation," she said. "This feels so great." She sighed as she leaned over to extract something from her bag. "One for you." She handed him something he didn't understand. "One for me."

Teagan watched her unfold the apparatus to reveal the back to a chair. He did the same, hoping he wasn't too oblivious in his experience with beach tools, tips, and tricks.

But of course he was.

"It just goes in the sand like this," she said, stabbing the ends of it down into the beach at the top of her towel. "And you can sit up and lean back." She did, beaming at him.

"Amazing," he said, copying her and sitting beside her. A long sigh leaked from his mouth too, and he closed his eyes and tipped his face toward the sun. Everything was golden and bright and hot, and Teagan's soul felt like he could soak it in forever.

"So nice, right?" she asked with a giggle.

"Amazing," he said, basking in the warmth, the company, the sound of surf and children laughing and everything about this moment. "I see why people do this now."

"Have you never laid on the beach?"

"It's been a while," he admitted. "But of course I have. At some point in the past, I have."

"You grew up here. What did you do as a child?"

"We came to the beach when Mother wanted to," he

said. "Usually on midweek afternoons. That's when there weren't as many tourists."

"What did your mother do?" Gwen asked.

"Nothing," Teagan said. "She lived on my dad's life insurance and her family's money. Her parents are very wealthy."

"Are your grandparents still alive?"

"Oh, no," he said. "My grandfather died several years ago." Teagan hadn't been particularly close to them. His mother had few friends, and while he knew she was lonely, he couldn't bring himself to do much about it. She'd done the same with her parents, and he supposed the cycle would have to be broken at some point.

"So do you have a lot of money?" Gwen asked, and Teagan turned toward her.

"Enough," he said. "You should know. You sign my checks."

"Uh, you have direct deposit," she teased. "And if we were living in the Dark Ages, Olympia would sign those checks."

Teagan laughed, squeezed her fingers, and said, "I'm so glad you invited me."

"Me too," Gwen said while giggling. "Me too." She leaned over and kissed him, and Teagan kept it chaste and quick, so he wouldn't get yelled at by a mother there with her kids.

"You're wearing that?" Gwen's voice made Teagan look down at his clothes. The passage between the two rooms was narrow, comprising of a few feet and through two doorways.

"Yes." He'd packed a pair of black slacks and this polo precisely for dinner with his family. "What's wrong with it?"

"You told me something nice." She gestured to her dress, which was *very* nice. Very nice indeed, what with the dark blue fabric hugging her body and swelling in all the right places.

"That is nice," he said, not quite getting why she was upset.

"It's too nice." She turned back to her bedroom, and Teagan followed her into it. "I didn't pack anything else." She started rifling through her suitcase, which she'd set on the luggage rack. Teagan saw at least three more bikini tops get shuffled around before he wrapped his arms around her from behind.

She straightened and stilled in his embrace. "It's fine," he said softly, touching his lips to the back of her neck. It was totally her fault for enticing him this way by pulling all of her hair into that sexy up-do.

"Teagan," she said playfully.

"What?" He pressed another kiss along her shoulder, where a very thin strap kept her dress up.

"We'll be late."

"No, we won't," he said. "We don't have to leave for ten

minutes."

She leaned back into his touch, and Teagan liked the silky smooth quality of her skin, the way she swayed with him as if they were slow dancing, and the powdery, rosy scent of her hair.

"And you don't need to change," he said. "Do you think I'm not dressed up enough?"

"I'll admit I was expecting a tie," she said, clutching his fingers with hers and turning toward him. "Did you bring one?"

Teagan didn't want to admit it, but he had. "You think I should wear it?"

"From what you've said about your mother, I'd definitely wear it."

"Fine," Teagan said, some bite to his tone that wasn't directed toward Gwen. "I need to change then." He went back through the doorway to his room, pulling his polo over his head. He had brought a baby blue dress shirt and a tie with lots of stripes on it. His mother loved stripes, and he sort of hated that he'd brought it just to make her happy.

But something down deep inside him wanted his mother to be happy, and Gwen must have picked up on that. He buttoned his shirt as Gwen came into the room, and she stepped up to him and began tying his tie for him.

The action was one of the sexiest moments of Teagan's life, and he stood there with this gorgeous woman only inches in front of him, her delicate fingers brushing his skin as she finished buttoning his top button and then began knotting his necktie. He could only watch her, his heart beating too fast and his fingers clenching into fists.

"There," she said, patting his chest right over the tie. She looked up at him, and so much was said in those few seconds. She must've been able to see something in his eyes, because a hint of a blush filled her cheeks and desire brimmed in her eyes.

She backed up a step, and then another, ducking her head and reaching up to tuck her hair. But it was already all pinned up, and she let her hand drop to her side.

"We better go," he whispered. "Before I ruin your lipstick."

She nodded and didn't wait for him to open the door to the hallway. He followed her, catching her hand in his as they walked to the elevator.

The restaurant Tilly had chosen was a short five-minute walk from their hotel, and Teagan caught sight of his sister through the window as they walked toward the front door.

"Are you ready for this?" he asked, pausing with his hand on the door.

Gwen smiled up at him. "This is going to be great, Teagan. You'll see."

"I guess we will see." He opened the door, the lilting music and chattery din of the restaurant spilling onto the sidewalk. His mother rose from the bench just inside the door, and the game was on.

13

Gwen stepped into a completely new skin as she walked through the door. She'd seen Olympia do it several times, and she believed she could charm his mother and his sister too.

"You must be Beverly." She took both of Teagan's mother's hands in her own and gave her kiss on each cheek. "I'm Gwen Heartwood."

"Oh," she said, letting Gwen lead the way. She glanced at Teagan, who smiled at his mother. Gwen could see the strain around his eyes, but he moved into his mother and gave her a hug as a pair of blonde girls came around the corner.

"Uncle Teagan," one of them said, and Gwen stayed with his mother as he moved over to his nieces.

"Are you Jill or Jenny?" he teased. "It doesn't matter. I'll just call you JJ." He hugged them both at the same time, laughter coming from his throat as he lifted them off the ground. They squealed and held onto his shoulders until he set them down.

"Teagan," his sister said as she arrived, and she hugged him too, a genuine smile on her face from what Gwen could tell.

And then everyone faced her. Teagan moved back to her side, easily putting his arm around her. "This is Gwen Heartwood," he said. "Gwen, my sister Tilly and her husband John. Their little girls Jill and Jenny. My mother, Beverly."

"Is she your girlfriend, Uncle Teagan?" one of the twins asked.

"She sure is." Teagan grinned at the girl, and Gwen shook hands with Tilly and John.

"We have a table back here," Tilly said, half-turning away from the group. She hadn't received Gwen in a particularly warm manner, but they were standing in the lobby of a restaurant.

"Front and center," Teagan muttered as they approached the table. "And why was my mother sitting in the lobby if we had a table already?"

Gwen didn't have time to answer, and she waited for Teagan to pull her chair out for her before she sat. They were indeed in the middle of the table, with Tilly and John across from them. The girls were separated on either side of their parents, and Teagan's mother sat next to him.

No one said a word. Gwen glanced down at the menu, and then looked at Teagan's sister. "So, what's good here?"

John started detailing a steak while Tilly helped the daughter next to her with the menu.

"And I like the lobster macaroni and cheese," Tilly said with a smile once her husband stopped talking.

"That sounds delicious," Gwen said.

"So you're a chef too," his mother said, and Gwen nodded.

"Yes," Teagan said. "I work at Gwen's inn."

"She owns the inn?"

"No," Gwen said quickly. "I don't own the inn. I mean, I have shares in the company."

"You do?" Teagan asked, and Gwen glanced at him.

"Yes," she said. "Sixteen percent." She plucked her napkin from the table and laid it in her lap. "Olympia runs the company, and she has the largest share. But it's still not even half, and she can't really make unilateral decisions without the rest of us."

"Us?" Tilly asked.

"Oh, my sisters," Gwen said quickly. "There are five of us. My oldest sister runs the inn, for the most part. I'm just over dining services."

"Which is a huge job," Teagan said. "Honestly, huge."

"I know you work a lot, dear," his mother said as the waiter arrived. He asked for drinks, and Gwen really wanted something to help numb her mind. But she wasn't a drinker, and she wasn't going to make a fool of herself tonight.

She ordered a respectable soda and turned to the girl on her side of the table. "What are you going to get?"

The girl cowered into her mother, her blue eyes round. "Chicken fingers."

Gwen gave her a small smile and turned toward Teagan, whose hand had just landed on her knee. She caught his mother saying, "...why you can't come visit more often."

"I have a job, Mother," he said.

"It's my fault," Gwen said. "I schedule Teagan seven nights a week at the inn, especially during our busy season. He really is the best chef on the island of Carter's Cove."

"Perhaps you went there because you couldn't get a job here," Beverly said, and even Gwen gasped. "There are always jobs here."

"I didn't apply for any jobs here," Teagan said.

"He could get them," Gwen said.

"He could, Mom," Tilly said. "Let this go."

"Why should I let it go?" She glared at Tilly. "My only son chose to live somewhere else when he could easily live here. There must be a reason."

Tilly glanced at Gwen, and entire lifetimes of conversations were had in that moment. "We're very happy to have him at The Heartwood Inn," Gwen said. "Have you ever been to Carter's Cove?"

"Why would I need to go to Carter's Cove?" Beverly demanded. "I live on an island."

"Maybe to visit Teagan," Gwen said, immediately regretting it. "Come see what he does. Check out our beaches." Gwen shrugged and picked up the menu. "Ooh, look, Teagan, they have fried calamari. Let's get that and see if it's as good as we do at the inn."

"Deal," Teagan said. "I'm also going to get the bruschetta. I think they do something different with their spices here I want you to try."

"And we'll get the garlic toast," Tilly said. "Sound good, John?"

"Amazing," he said, and the waiter arrived with their drinks, causing further distance from his mother's awkward conversation. They ordered appetizers, and Gwen asked, "John, what do you do for a living? I don't think Teagan has said."

"I'm the lead project manager for an insurance company."

Gwen nodded like she had any idea what that meant. Tilly actually started laughing. "No one knows what that means," she said.

"I do," Teagan said. "I mean, I'm the lead project manager for a huge hotel chain on an island." He chuckled as John did. "What? It's true."

"I deal with marketing for the company," John said. "We're always looking for something better than a gecko, you know?"

Gwen laughed, glad Tilly and John seemed normal, at least. Beverly hadn't said another word, and a quick glance at her showed her sulking on the other side of Teagan. Great. Gwen searched for a way to bring her back into the conversation. What would Olympia do? Her mother?

"Beverly," she said. "What do you spend your time doing?"

"I went to the laundromat today," she said.

Gwen looked at Teagan, who simply lifted one shoulder in a very slight shrug.

"And I like reading," Beverly said. "Do you read, Gwen?"

"Oh, no, ma'am," Gwen said with a chuckle. "I don't have much time for leisure reading."

"Reading keeps your brain active," Beverly said.

"I'm sure it does," Gwent said. "What do you like to read?"

"A little of this," she said at the same time Tilly said, "She likes romance novels."

"Oh, Tilly." Beverly smiled though, and she didn't argue.

"I like romance novels too," Gwen said. "Everything works out in the end, you know?"

"Oh, I read three per week," Tilly said. "Because you're right. I like how everyone gets their kiss in the end." She smiled around at everyone and opened her mouth to ask Gwen another question.

Gwen didn't hear her because Beverly had also spoken.

"Mom," Teagan said, but Gwen hadn't caught what his mother had said.

"I'm sorry, what?"

"I asked if you two wanted children," Beverly said, and Gwen distinctly saw Tilly shake her head.

"Well, yeah," Gwen said at the same time Teagan said, "No."

Surprise filled her with a single breath. "No?"

"Don't engage," Tilly said. "Teagan, tell us how you and Gwen met."

Teagan held Gwen's gaze for another moment. Then another. Then he looked at his sister and said, "She owns the inn where I work," his voice filled with nothing but ice.

By the time Gwen finished dinner and had given her good-byes to Teagan's family, she felt wrung out and upside down. She and Teagan gave one final wave to Tilly and her family, and then Gwen wished they'd driven though their hotel was only a couple of blocks away. He'd shut down pretty heavily after his mother had asked about children, and Gwen couldn't get the word *no* out of her head. With Tilly's help, she'd managed to keep the conversation going, and she was utterly exhausted.

She pressed her fingertips together and closed her eyes briefly. Teagan walked beside her, utterly silent.

"You don't want kids," Gwen said to break the ice. She wasn't asking.

"No," he said without looking at her. He seemed to be walking really fast, and Gwen couldn't quite keep up in her heels. She didn't wear shoes like this every day, and this stroll back to the hotel wasn't anything like the slow, sensual one they'd taken to get here.

She wanted to lace her arm through his and discuss what dinner had been like, how great his sister was, and that yes, his mother was a little overbearing, but she was still a wonderful lady.

"I have a daughter," he finally said when the neon lights of their hotel came into view. "And I'm a terrible father to her, and I don't need to repeat that again."

"It wouldn't be the same at all," Gwen said, though he hadn't said anything about Abby since telling her about his daughter when they'd first gotten back together.

"Why wouldn't it?" Teagan glared at her out of the corner of his eye.

"We would be together," Gwen said. "We'd be building our family together."

Teagan shook his head. "That's what I thought with Caroline, and it didn't work out."

"Are you saying you think we wouldn't work out?" Gwen asked.

"I'm saying I don't want children," Teagan said. "I don't

know how to be a father, and I'm not interested in...going through all of that again."

"All of what?" Gwen asked. "You've never really said what happened."

"The guilt," he said. "The regret. The second-guessing." He stopped suddenly and faced her, his eyes storming and angry. "I did what I thought was right, and that was to walk away. Caroline didn't need me, and I didn't know she was pregnant at the time. I was nineteen years old."

Agony mixed with fury in his voice, and Gwen had no idea what to say to get him to calm down, to soothe him somehow. She also had no idea what he'd gone through—what he was still going through—when it came his daughter.

"You're not nineteen years old now," she said, the words coming into her mind. "You're not the same person you were then. Why do you think anything would be the same?"

He visibly softened, but only a little bit. "Can we talk about this in the morning? I don't want to say something I'll regret later."

"Of course." Gwen put her arm through his. "But can we walk slower? These heels are killing me."

Teagan did slow down then, but he still didn't say anything. He unlocked his room and led her inside, and he kissed her quickly in their shared doorway. He was loosening his tie when she went into her bedroom, and she heard his side of the door close only a couple of seconds after hers did.

"Well," she whispered to herself as she shimmied out of her slinky dress. "You survived the dinner with his family." Now she just had to weather the aftermath of it.

14

Teagan tossed in bed for a solid hour before he got up. He left his room quietly, because it was after hours, and he didn't want anyone to call down to the front desk and complain about a guest on the fifteenth floor. Not when Gwen had gotten the rooms at the last minute from a friend.

He cringed at the dinging of the elevator, but no one rushed out of their rooms to shush him. He made it to the lobby and out the beach exit, which was clearly marked. He double-checked to make sure he had his keycard to get back in, and his phone. Then he just walked.

His mind churned at a blistering pace, but he couldn't pull out any of the individual thoughts. The sky spread above him, with lots of lights bordering the walkway to his left and none out on the ocean to his right. He'd left without shoes, so he went down to the hard-packed sand to walk, his feet eating up the yards easily.

When he realized he couldn't see any lights on his left, he paused. "What am I supposed to do?" He couldn't help his feelings of failure when it came to his experiences in fatherhood.

But he'd made those decisions for himself, based on his situation. Things probably would be different with Gwen—with any woman where he had a mature, loving relationship.

And to do that, he had to be honest. Open. And communicate. He hadn't done any of those things with Caroline, or Abby to a large extent. He'd been getting better and better, and he thought he had a decent relationship with his daughter now.

But he hadn't spoken to Caroline in several years. He couldn't imagine not talking to Gwen for even a day, though he had had a few months there where his own communication with her was work-related. But he still spoke to her.

Teagan held very still and let his feelings swell and move through him. He didn't want to shut Gwen out, and he didn't want to lose her over this issue.

"Gotta go talk to her." He'd be shocked if she'd been able to fall asleep, and he pulled out his phone. *Hey, are you still awake?*

I went for a walk, but when I get back, can we talk?

Her response came only a few seconds later. *Sure, just*

knock on my door.

Satisfied, and now suddenly anxious to get their talk over so he could sleep, he strode back toward the hotel down the beach. He'd gone farther than he'd thought, and thirty minutes had passed before he arrived back in his room, slightly out of breath and his calves aching from walking without shoes.

He took a minute to wet a washcloth with cold water and wipe his face before he moved over to her closed door and tapped on it. Several long seconds passed before she opened the door, and she stood there in front of him in a tiny pair of shorts and a gray T-shirt that was two sizes too big.

She was still breathtakingly beautiful, and Teagan blurted, "I'm sorry."

"For what?" She curled her fingers around the door and cocked one hip into it.

"For getting angry at dinner. For shutting down for a little bit. For being a bad father."

She sighed. "You're not a bad father."

"You don't even know," he said, shaking his head. "It's fine. That's not what matters. What matters here is that you might be right."

"Is that so?" she asked, a softness entering her gaze.

"I mean, maybe," he said. "It's hard for me to say, but I think everything would be different in a marriage to a woman I actually love."

She tilted her head and backed up. "You want to

come in?"

He did, letting her door close behind him gently. "I didn't love Caroline. I loved the idea of being in love, and she was an actress." He hated the words as they left his mouth, but they were true. "I'm not the same person I was twenty years ago."

"None of us are," she said.

"That's because you were ten years old," he teased. "And thank goodness you're not the same now as you were then."

"I do still like banana splits," she said. "And it sure is taking a long time for the one I ordered from room service to show up."

"You ordered from room service?"

"As soon as you texted," she said. "Some conversations go better with ice cream." She crawled onto the bed she was obviously going to sleep in, and Teagan perched on the other one.

"So, because you're right, I'm willing to be open to discussing having children."

Someone knocked on the door as soon as he finished speaking, and Gwen launched herself off the bed and over to the door. "Thank you," she said. "Yes, right in here is fine."

A man entered with a tray in his hand and set it on the desk before turning back to Gwen, who handed him a bill before he left. The door closed, and she said, "Okay, time for ice cream."

"Did you hear what I said?" Teagan asked, rising.

"Yes," she said, finally looking at him with a measure of desire in her eyes. "And I appreciate it. You're not the only one to blame, though. I have no right to assume how things will go, and I can't judge how you feel, because I haven't lived your past."

Teagan nodded, what she'd said so kind. Just so, so kind. "Thank you. I might not want to talk about it, but I'm willing to consider having kids."

"That's fine for now," she said. "We've just started seeing each other." She stepped up to him and cradled his face in one hand while the other snaked around the back of his neck and gently pressed until his head lowered and touched they touched foreheads. "Okay?"

"Okay," he whispered. "Sorry to keep you up so late."

"And we haven't even started the banana split yet," she said, her smile touching his mouth as she kissed him.

TEAGAN WOKE IN THE MORNING WHEN A DOOR SLAMMED somewhere. He'd silenced his phone when he'd finally returned from the late-night dessert party in Gwen's room. They'd agreed to a late start that day, but no time had been set. She had a habit of rising early, same as him, but surely she'd sleep in a little bit. He hadn't left her room until almost one-thirty in the morning.

He groaned as he sat up, his back not appreciating the

hardness of this mattress. After scrubbing his hands through his hair, he reached for his phone. He had a few messages from Gwen, the last one reading, *I'm headed out for breakfast. I'm waking you up when I get back.*

"Holy cow," he said when he saw the time. It was after ten-thirty. No wonder she wanted to get going. He tapped out a quick message to say he was up and getting in the shower. Then he jumped over to his suitcase and pulled out his toiletries before going into the bathroom to get ready.

Twenty minutes later, he answered the door to a fun, flirty Gwen wearing a beach hat and carrying two to-go cups of coffee and a white pastry bag. "There better be raspberry fritters in there," he said.

"Two," she said with a smile. She tipped up onto her toes and kissed him quickly before coming into his room. "And we can eat on the beach or right here. What would you like?"

"The beach," he said, not wanting to spend any time in this hotel room if he could help it. "But weren't we going out to Lookout Point today?"

"Yes, so let's eat and go." She stepped over to the doors that bridged the gap between their rooms. "I'll grab my beach bag."

Teagan picked up the pastries and coffee and followed her, finding her with that brightly colored beach bag that she'd packed and brought down to the sand yesterday too. "Ready?"

"So ready," she said, watching him. "You must've been tired."

"I was," he said. "I think in more ways than one."

"I'm glad you got to rest," she said, and Teagan could hear the genuine quality of her voice.

Downstairs, they found a table on the outdoor patio, which wasn't hard as it was nearly lunchtime and all the breakfast-goers had cleared out already. He snacked on his raspberry fritter and sipped his coffee and listened to Gwen tell stories of her sisters growing up at The Heartwood Inn.

"And there were all these secret passages at the inn," she said. "Once, Sheryl locked me inside one, and I freaked out."

"Really? That doesn't seem like Sheryl."

"She was different as a teenager," Gwen said. "Trust me."

"Define freaked out," Teagan said.

"Oh, I was eleven, and I was crying and screaming and when my dad finally heard me, we were in so much trouble." She giggled and shook her head.

"I like these stories." He watched a family go by, their three children each carrying beach gear as they went down the sidewalk. The little girl called for her brother to help her as she dropped a bucket of plastic toys, and the boy turned back. The mother and father went on, but Teagan caught the mom looking to make sure her kids would catch up.

Their chubby hands picked up the toys and put them in the bucket, and then they ran to catch the other people in their family. Teagan smiled at them, enjoying the innocence of them.

"Sounds like you had a good time growing up with your sisters," he said.

"There were moments." Gwen smiled at him. "This beach feels less frantic than ours."

"It's just as busy," he said. "It might be because you don't have to worry about getting a text that will cause you to run back inside and solve a problem."

She smiled at him and leaned her head against his bicep. "I think that's it."

He pressed a kiss to the top of her head. "You ready to go to Lookout Point? You can sometimes see whales there."

"Not in the middle of the day," she said. "Right?"

"Yeah, probably not. I don't know," he said. "Maybe we'll get lucky." Teagan already felt pretty lucky, and he hoped he wouldn't do or say anything else to ruin the next ten days. He had very few things in his life that were important to him, and he had to fight for the ones that were.

And he'd realized in the past few days that Gwen was on that list, and he might have some work to do on himself to be the man Gwen needed. But he was willing to do it.

15

"It's right there," Gwen said, pointing. "See the tailfin?"

"I see it," Teagan said excitedly. "There *is* a whale there."

They'd stopped for lunch on the way out to Lookout Point, and by the time they'd walked up the path to the highest point overlooking the water, the sun had started to arc down in the west. Gwen hadn't had such a relaxing day in ages, and she wanted another one like today. And then another. And then another.

The whale's tail came up again, and Gwen smiled at the simple beauty of it. The very real feeling of Teagan beside her, despite their differences. The wind blew off the ocean and into her face, and she breathed in the salty scent of it.

"Do you want to go down to the shops?" Teagan asked after they'd stood there for several minutes.

"Yes," Gwen said at the same time her phone chimed. She glanced at it and choked. "Oh, my goodness. It's Celeste. I have to call her." She jabbed at the phone icon at the top of the screen, ignoring Teagan's question of "What's wrong?"

Celeste answered the phone with a squeal, and Gwen really wished she was there. "You really booked Georgia Panic?"

"We said we weren't working for the next ten days," Teagan said, looking very stern. Gwen held up one finger, because this was *Georgia Panic*, one of the best bands in the *world*. And maybe Gwen had a little crush on their drummer. A tiny little crush, from way last year.

"I really did," Celeste said, laughing. "And not only that, but they want a friends and family dinner catered, *and* they want a catered fan event."

Gwen didn't have their calendar memorized, but Celeste had access to it. "Does it work with the schedule?"

"It sure does," she said gleefully. "How's your trip so far?"

She looked at Teagan's back as he walked away from her. "I have to go, actually. Can I call you later?"

"If you don't, I will be so mad," Celeste said, and Gwen laughed with her.

She hung up and called, "Teagan," after him. He paused but didn't turn to look at her. "It wasn't really work," she said as she caught up to him. "Celeste did book Georgia Panic, but it was more of a sister fangirl moment."

"You like Georgia Panic." He wasn't asking, and he didn't look amused.

"Yeah," Gwen said. "Are you going to be mad over a thirty-second phone call?" She ran her fingertips up his arm. "I thought we were going shopping. I want to buy all kinds of stupid souvenirs for my sisters." She smiled at him, and he took the glaring down a couple of notches. "And maybe I have—*had*—a crush on the Panic drummer."

She shrugged one shoulder like anything was possible.

"Oh, I see." He grinned at her, his bad mood gone now. "All right, let's go shopping," he said.

"And we can look for somewhere good to eat dinner."

He smiled at her then, and Gwen knew she was forgiven for the "business" phone call.

"It is nice not having to think about work," she said.

"So nice," he agreed.

"Do you ever wish you'd done something else with your life?" she asked.

"I don't know what I would've done."

"Have you always wanted to be a chef?"

"Yes," he said.

"Me too," she said. "I used to get kitchen items for Christmas. Pots and pans and knives. I was cooking family dinner when I was twelve years old." Gwen smiled at the memories.

"Me too," he said. "But out of necessity, not because I particularly enjoyed it."

"But you do enjoy it now, right?" She'd seen his interaction with his mother, and she wasn't surprised he'd been cooking since childhood. A pang of sadness hit her though, because her experiences in the kitchen were filled with joy and love, not bitterness and resentment.

"Yeah," he said. "But honestly, I went to culinary school to prove to my mother that she couldn't control me." He didn't sound happy about what he'd just said. "And because the institution I'd gotten into was all the way across the country from Caroline."

"What happened with her?" Gwen said as they reached the bottom of the steps. They'd have to drive back to the downtown area to shop out here on Lookout Point, so she headed for the car.

"She was a child actress," he said. "So she was already famous when I met her. And she was...charming. Beautiful. I was young and stupid. We both were, but especially me." He unlocked the car and held her door while she got in. Once he was seated behind the wheel, he said, "And like I said already, I loved the idea of us. So we got married on a whim. Her parents were *so* angry."

"I can imagine," Gwen said.

"They wanted an annulment, but Caroline fought them on it." He drove slowly out of the parking lot, and Gwen mentally said good-bye to the whales. "She was older than me, and there wasn't much her parents could do about the marriage. But the shininess of our relationship wore off pretty fast, and it was obvious we weren't going to stay married. So I left."

"And you found out about Abby later."

"Yes," he said. "Not until she was two years old, actually." His spoke in a very quiet voice, and Gwen took a few seconds to think about what that must've been like for him. No wonder he'd been beating himself up about it for the past twenty years.

"I didn't go back. I didn't meet her until I finished culinary school. She was three, and she had no idea who I was. It's been a difficult road for us, but I think we're doing okay now."

"I can't wait to meet her," Gwen said.

"Why would you need to meet her?" Teagan asked, glancing at Gwen.

"What?" Gwen searched his face, but he looked back out the windshield. "She's your *daughter*, Teagan. Of course I'm going to meet her."

"Maybe," he said.

"Why wouldn't I?"

"What if we don't work out?"

"You think we're not going to work out?" Gwen had no idea what to say to that. She'd invited him on a ten-day trip, for crying out loud. They were getting along great, in her opinion. They'd worked through a difficult conversation topic already, and she enjoyed spending time with him.

Except for right now, that was.

She hated this back and forth with Teagan. She felt like she was on a teeter-totter or playing a teenage game of *she loves him....she loves him not.*

And she wasn't in love with Teagan Hatch—and least not yet. But standing up on the lookout with him, watching that magnificent whale she could feel herself slipping in that direction. With every honest conversation they had, she inched further toward falling in love with him.

Every time he drank her up like he was so happy to see her, every time their hands touched, every time he kissed her with those slow, passionate movements, she fell a little further.

"I don't know, Gwen," he finally said. "Do we have to decide right now?"

"No," she said, her voice stung.

"I feel like I have a lot to work on," Teagan said, pressing his hands against his forehead. "I need to go see someone."

Gwen's eyebrows went up. "Like a counselor?"

"Exactly like that."

"Have you done that before?" she asked.

"Yes," he said. "Right after I found out about Abby. I had a lot of feelings during that time and talking them out with a neutral party helped a lot."

Gwen was sure it did. Being able to run things by Celeste had been important to Gwen for a long time. And she appreciated the candid way Teagan talked through hard things with her too.

He found a parking spot on the street, but Gwen didn't feel much merriment as she got out to go shopping. "How will you know when I can meet Abby?" she asked, peering down the road. A bus sat parked next to a boutique, freshly painted but obviously not going anywhere. School Bus Ice Cream the sign proudly proclaimed, and Gwen suddenly needed something sweet.

"I don't know," he said. "I guess I'll just know."

"Has she ever met any of your girlfriends?" Gwen asked. She'd never seen Teagan take a day off before, so she knew he hadn't flown to California to visit his daughter in at least five years. Probably longer.

"No," Teagan said. "I haven't had many of those, and no."

So she'd be the first of his girlfriends to meet Abby. It was suddenly a very big job, and Gwen wasn't sure she was up to the task. After all, the woman was only ten years younger than her. How could she ever be a mother figure for her?

Gwen didn't ask him any more questions after that. Teagan tended to shut down on topics he wasn't interested in talking about, but he usually came around. Abby seemed to be particularly off-limits, though, and Gwen wondered if she was kidding herself when it came to Teagan.

He'd never seemed like he needed more in his life

than he currently had, even when they hadn't been on good speaking terms. She felt like she was asking a lot of him, almost like she wanted him to be someone he wasn't. Not only that, but someone he wasn't capable of becoming. Or someone he didn't want to become.

Gwen poked through shops and bought a couple of hand-thrown mugs by local Whistlestop Shores artists for Celeste and Olympia, both of whom loved coffee and tea almost as much as life itself. She found a pair of earrings for Sheryl in the shape of potted plants and a pair of fishing gloves for Alissa.

She wanted something for her parents and grandmother too, but they had plenty of time to visit more shops on the Shores.

Teagan didn't say much as she exclaimed over trinkets, bought magnets for her fridge, and asked him where he wanted to eat. A tension existed between them now, and Gwen really just wanted twenty-four hours where they could just be together without the underlying anxiety.

"Take me somewhere you liked as a kid," she said. "Or a teenager. Whatever."

"I didn't like Whistlestop Shores growing up," he said, almost roughly.

"Nothing about it?"

"Very little," he said.

"Then take me to the little you did like."

He looked at her, and so many storms swirled in those eyes that had always captivated her. Frustration filled his gaze, and Gwen felt it stirring in her soul too. Why was being with him so hard? And being without him was torture.

But did she really want the rest of her life to be filled with this constant rift? This tension? This up and down and around emotional roller coaster?

"I'd rather make our own memories here," he finally said. "Good ones, that we only know about."

And he always had the perfect thing to say. At least it felt that way to Gwen. "Okay," she said. "What do you feel like eating tonight?" They'd had fancy food at the restaurant last night, and that was forty-five minutes around the island, back where their hotel waited for them.

"There's a great crab shack right around here," he said. "At least, I've heard Tilly talk about it. It wasn't here when we were kids."

"A new memory then," she said. "I like crab."

Teagan tapped and swiped on his phone, finally saying, "Here it is. Ten minutes away. Doable?"

"Yep," Gwen said, looking out her window. "Doable." What she wasn't sure was doable was dealing with Teagan's moods, his tightly held secrets, and his past for the rest of her life. But she'd already started to fall for him, and she didn't know how to claw her way back up the mountain now. She wasn't even sure she wanted to. So many things swirled inside her mind—inside Teagan's too, obviously, as neither of them said a word on the ten-minute drive to the crab shack.

She felt like she was holding tightly to a kite string while the wind whipped the toy back and forth through the tumultuous sky. And the worst part? Teagan held a pair of scissors and could cut her free at any time.

She'd go soaring up into the thunderclouds, getting zapped by lightning whenever she brought up a topic he didn't like, and then eventually, she'd fall, and there would be no one there to catch her.

16

Teagan scrubbed a towel through his hair and went into this hotel room. Gwen wanted to go to a farmer's market that morning, and Teagan wanted to spend time with Gwen. Dinner last night had been a tense affair, and they'd both retired early to their rooms.

He'd been up since dawn, and he'd seen Gwen's pictures on social media. Pictures of her down on the beach at night, eating gourmet chocolate from a food cart she'd found on the boardwalk—without him.

His chest had pinched, but they'd agreed they could have time to themselves if they needed it. And Gwen obviously needed it. On the second day.

Teagan knew why, but he wasn't sure how to take back the words he'd said about his daughter. He barely saw Abby, and he honestly hadn't thought he'd need to introduce her to Gwen. Or any woman, really.

He pulled out his phone and started a text to his daughter, though it would be way too early for Abby to respond right away. *Would you ever want to meet*

He didn't know how to finish the text. Meet who? The woman he loved? The woman he might marry? He wasn't sure Gwen was either of those things, at the moment. He really liked her, and he wanted to learn more about her. But he wasn't in love with her.

Though, if he was...he'd want to marry her.

His emotions went up and down, around and around, as if attached to a yo-yo. But they were going to the farmer's market in ten minutes, and he might need all of those to figure out what to text to his daughter.

He deleted what he'd already typed and tried again. If my girlfriend wanted to meet you, what would you think of that?

He pulled on a pair of board shorts and a T-shirt he hadn't worn yet, shoved his wallet in his back pocket, and sighed. His phone chimed a few times from its spot on the dresser, and he picked it up, expecting to see Gwen's name there.

But Abby had texted back already. Surprise moved through him from that, and from what she'd said. *First, you have a girlfriend? Is it that woman you texted me about a couple of weeks ago?*

Second, I want a picture of her right now.

Third, if you want me to meet her, I'd meet her.

So she'd left it up to him, but Teagan didn't have to decide right away. Abby lived clear across the country, and he wouldn't see her until the holidays at the earliest.

Dad, picture, Abby said, and Teagan started swiping through his picture gallery. He didn't have a single picture of Gwen. She'd been taking pictures of the two of them. Breakfast on the beach. Watching the whales. Dinner with his family. She posted way more on social media than he did, which wasn't hard. He couldn't even remember the last time he'd put a picture online, and he didn't have anything to send to Abby.

A few minutes later, Gwen knocked on the door separating their rooms. Teagan opened it, already saying, "Hey, so I need a picture—" His voice muted when he saw what Gwen was wearing.

The long, tropical dress covered a lot of her body, but not her slender, creamy shoulders. Her neck was exposed as she'd pulled her hair up on top of her head. She wore bright red lipstick and a pair of sunglasses and a smile.

"Ready for the farmer's market?" she asked. "And the beach?"

"Yes," he said through a dry throat. "You look great."

"I have my swimming suit on under this," she said. "It's just a cover-up."

"It's gorgeous." Teagan reached for her hand. "I texted Abby, and she said she'd like a picture of you. Us." Why was this so hard? He felt completely out of his league when it came to Gwen Heartwood. He felt like he should have more control over his emotions at almost forty years old, but he honestly felt like he couldn't take another step without the ground vanishing beneath his feet.

"But I don't have any," he continued when Gwen just stood there.

She finally lifted her sunglasses up, and their eyes met. "You want to send a picture of us to your daughter?"

"Yes, she asked for one."

Gwen nodded and started swiping on her phone. "I have the one of us at Lookout Pointe yesterday. Will that work?"

"Yes."

"Did you tell her about this trip?" Gwen didn't look at him as she continued to work on sending him the picture.

"No," he said.

"What did you say?"

"I asked her if she'd like to meet my girlfriend in the future, and she—"

"Wait." Gwen looked up at him. "You asked her if she'd like to meet me?"

"Yes." Teagan watched her, surprised to see a flush stain her cheeks. "I think it's obvious I have no idea what I'm doing, as a boyfriend or a father."

His phone chimed again, and she said, "That's the picture. What else did Abby ask?"

"She wanted a picture, and she said it was up to me if she met you."

"And?"

"And I think—" Teagan swept his hand through his

hair. "I think we'll probably be together during the holidays, and she'll be here then, and you should probably meet her."

Gwen tucked her phone back into her tiny purse and smiled. "I think we'll probably be together during the holidays too."

Teagan ducked his head as he smiled. "All right, then. Let's hit the farmer's market. I'm starving."

Gwen looped her arm through his, and they left the hotel together. The farmer's market was just down the street at a park, and Teagan could see the white tents from the sidewalk in front of the hotel.

"Abby loves a good farmer's market," he said.

"So do I," Gwen said. "But I like tons of stuff like this. I like the food truck rallies on the island. I like the surfing championships. I like the dog shows, and the beach nights, and the outdoor movies." She took in a deep breath. "It's the sense of community, I think, that I like."

"Carter's Cove has way better community than the Shores," he said. "At least I think so."

"I think so too," Gwen said. "But I can't wait to see what they have at this farmer's market."

"It's going to be the same overpriced stuff we found out at Lookout Pointe yesterday. You know that, right?"

Gwen giggled and skipped ahead of him. "Yeah, I know that. But there's going to be that crepe truck, and I've already picked out the one I want."

"I'm totally going to get two," Teagan said, the scent of

chocolate filling the air. They crossed the street and entered the park, the first booth Gwen saw intriguing her. She had to look at everything in the booth, which boasted homemade soaps that all smelled the same to Teagan. She bought a bubble brush, and they finally moved on. But the essential oils in the next tent captured her attention, and Teagan's stomach growled.

But he liked Gwen's enthusiasm—and the fact that the tension between them had disappeared. He learned she liked the scent of peppermint over lavender, and that flavored honeys were *not* acceptable, and that Gwen sure was amazing with talking to strangers.

She exuded happiness in a way Teagan had never experienced, but that he wanted to.

"Crepes," Gwen said, and Teagan gestured her toward the food truck with a few people lingering out front. She told him what she wanted, and Teagan ordered for both of them.

They finally got their food, and Teagan did order two. He couldn't decide between a savory or a sweet one, and the one with banana, coconut, and caramel was amazing. As was the one with scrambled eggs, bacon, and avocado mayo.

Gwen got berries and cream, and he had a bite of hers too. As the sun heated the day, their time at the farmer's market ended. "Time to go to the beach?"

"Definitely," he said, because he really wanted to see what swimming suit she was wearing under that coverup.

It must not have straps, because her shoulders were very bare.

Sunday at the beach was busy, but with school in, it wasn't as bad as it could've been. Gwen found them a spot, and she pulled a blanket from the beach bag she'd been carrying around all morning.

She sighed as she sat down, and Teagan did too. The sound of the waves coming ashore soothed him, and Teagan reached over to hold her hand. "Thanks for being patient with me."

"We all have things we need to work on," she said.

Teagan thought that was probably true, but he felt particularly broken. He closed his eyes and tried to find a time in his life he could classify himself as happy. His mother had not been ideal, and certainly nothing like how Gwen had grown up.

He'd gone as far from Whistlestop Shores as he could get, but he'd screwed up in California too. So he'd retreated and worked for a couple of years to save for culinary school, because he'd lost his place at the one in California when he'd married Caroline.

When he had enough money, he attended an institute in Kansas, which wasn't as prestigious as a lot of people. Most chefs, actually.

He'd come back to the East Coast because he wanted a job at a beach resort. He'd worked at two before The Heartwood Inn, and he definitely liked Heartwood the best. He didn't know how to be a dad, and he'd never really tried, if he were being honest with himself. At least not until Abby got older, got a phone, and his communication with her became easier for them both.

And then everything had happened with Gwen, and he'd panicked because he had no idea how to be a boyfriend or a father. At least he wasn't a liar too.

Teagan told himself to *take one day at a time*. One conversation. One situation. He was getting better at expressing himself, and if Gwen would continue to be patient with him, maybe this relationship would work out.

17

Gwen enjoyed the next several days with Teagan. She didn't bring up his daughter, or his family, or anything that required a hard conversation to be had. Honestly, she was exhausted with all they'd already talked about, and she couldn't imagine how Teagan felt.

He didn't bring up anything of importance, unless talking her through how beach volleyball was scored as they watched game after sandy game during the championships on Saturday afternoon and evening.

The following morning, they were headed back to Carter's Cove, and then it was back to business as usual at The Heartwood Inn bright and early on Monday morning.

Gwen was proud of herself for only checking in with Gordon once, Olympia a couple of times, and Bea a few times. She and Teagan had agreed to some time apart, and he didn't get to decide what she did with her free time.

Sunday dawned with Gwen standing on the beach, the waves flowing gently over her bare feet. She held her sandals in her fingers and bathed in the golden sunlight as it breathed life into a new day.

She filled her lungs with air again and again and looked up into the sky. Not a cloud sat there, and she wished she felt as tranquil as the landscape around her. She wasn't even sure what festered inside her. Simply that something did.

Eventually, she made her way back to her room and started to pack. She and Teagan were meeting for breakfast at nine, and then they'd drive home. She was planning to spend the afternoon in Celeste's office, telling her everything about the last ten days as her sister prepped for the week's events at the inn.

Fine, she might go into the kitchen and spend some time behind her own desk too. She hadn't decided that yet. What she really wanted to do was eat dinner with Teagan at Redfin. A meal they didn't make and hadn't engineered.

"Hey," she said when Teagan came into her room. "I'm almost ready. Listen." She turned toward him and smiled as she ran his palms up his chest. "How about dinner at Redfin tonight?"

His eyebrows went up, and Gwen found him so, so handsome. She wasn't sure exactly what love felt like, but she was pretty sure she was dangerously close to falling all the way in love with him.

"Redfin? Really?"

"Yeah," she said, tipping up to kiss him quickly. She didn't move away very far before adding, "A meal we don't have to make at our own restaurant. We'll just order the special, which you didn't have to come up with or teach to anyone else." Her lips curved up at the same time his did.

"Sounds great." He leaned his forehead against hers. "I've sure enjoyed this trip with you."

"Me too," she said, letting the soft moment lengthen between them. "Okay." She drew in a breath and stepped back. "Let me finish packing, and then you can haul my bag down to the car."

Teagan chuckled as she stepped into her sandals and tossed her toiletry bag into her suitcase. A zip up later, and she was ready. They went downstairs, where he put their bags in the trunk of the car, and then he took her hand in his.

"I know eggs aren't your favorite food, but there's a great place I used to like as a kid."

"Okay," Gwen said as casually as she could. He hadn't said anything else about this island where he'd grown up since the very beginning of their trip, and somehow that had only stoked Gwen's curiosity about him.

"They have other stuff too," he said. "Don't let the name fool you."

"What's it called?"

"Ham Over Eggs," he said. "They have great bagel breakfast sandwiches."

"Is that what you got as a kid?"

"No, it's what I created for their menu as a teenager. Ham Over Eggs was my first paying job as a sixteen-year-old."

Gwen blinked and then burst out laughing. "I can't wait to go, then."

"I don't work there now," he said.

"Still," she said. "Do you know how rare it is to have your creation on a menu, Teagan? It's awesome."

"I guess," he said, and Gwen shook his head as they continued walking down the street. Ham Over Eggs was a couple of blocks down, and a giant fried egg broadcasted its location.

"Wow," she said. "That's...a big egg."

Teagan laughed and squeezed her hand. "I tried to redesign the branding too, but no one listened to me."

"Is it locally owned?"

"Would a chain have a twenty-foot egg outside?"

"Point taken." They arrived at the breakfast joint, and Teagan opened the door for her. The scent of eggs hit Gwen full in the nose, which was probably a good thing for a restaurant with an overeasy egg on a pole out front. But Gwen didn't like eggs all that much, and she almost turned around and left.

"Not sure it smelled like this when I worked here," Teagan said, frowning as he came in after her. "Smells like someone put a pan of eggs on the burner and walked away for too long."

At least she wasn't the only one put off by the smell. She let Teagan go in front of her as they approached the counter. If she'd come to Whistlestop Shores, she wouldn't have picked this place to eat. She liked to be seated and served, and while she didn't have anything against establishments that had customers order and then sit down with a number, it wasn't her jam.

But Teagan had barely arrived at the counter when someone said, "Teagan Hatch," with a healthy dose of laughter following. An older man came around the counter and embraced Teagan, still laughing with that smile on his face.

"Alan," Teagan said, accepting the hug and pounding heartily on the other man's back. "You're still here."

"I bought this place," Alan said. "Right after you left, actually."

Teagan said something Gwen didn't catch, but Alan didn't seem to understand the meaning of the word quiet or whisper, because his voice was just as boisterous as before when he said, "Nothing to apologize for, Teagan. Nothing at all. You want one of your sandwiches? I kept them all on the menu."

Teagan stepped back to Gwen and put his hand in hers. "Alan, this is my girlfriend, Gwen."

"Oh." Alan blinked, clear shock moving across his

face. Gwen wondered what that was about, but she just extended her free hand to him.

"Nice to meet you," she said, putting her professional, plastic smile on her face.

Alan lunged forward as if someone had pushed him. He grabbed onto her hand and said, "Yes, yes, nice to meet you too. How's your daughter?"

Gwen's smile slipped and she looked at Teagan, who looked like he'd been sucker-punched.

"This isn't Abby's mother," he said.

"Oh." Alan looked back and forth between Teagan and Gwen. "I just thought...you always said.... Never mind. Come order." He bustled around the counter and positioned himself behind the cash register. When he looked at them again, all traces of his surprise had vanished.

Gwen really wanted to ask what Teagan had always said, but she looked up to the menu and found the Ham and Hatch Sandwiches. There were six listed, and they all screamed Teagan, what with their poppyseed buns and mustard aiolis.

"I'll have the Triple T," she said. "Is that T for Teagan?"

"Maybe," he said with a smile that seemed a little strained around the edges. Of course it was. He'd been standing right here when Alan had thought she was his daughter's mother.

What had he always said?

"Dinner at seven?" he asked later, as he placed her suitcase just inside her front door.

"Yep," she said. "I'll already be at the inn. I'm meeting my sister there this afternoon."

"I'll see you then."

She leaned into his kiss, and she waved as he sighed and backed away before turning to return to his car. He drove away, and Gwen went inside and closed the door. Midnight and Joey had come to greet her, but she couldn't bring herself to bend down and pat them. Midnight kept jumping on her, and finally Gwen leaned down and said hello.

"Did you guys miss me?" she asked. "Did you? Didn't Celeste play with you? Didn't she?"

The dogs finally calmed, and Gwen looked around the house. It looked the same as always. The air conditioning blew. The sun shone in the windows. For some reason, she expected things to be different. She felt so different than she had ten days ago.

After towing her suitcase down the hall and into her bedroom, she returned to the kitchen and scooped the tiny black dog into her arms. "Come on, guys. Let's go sit on the porch."

She had missed her time in the evenings with the dogs. They were good friends, and they were always happy to see her, and they didn't have a hard time expressing their feelings.

Midnight curled up on her lap, and Joey jumped up

right next to her, putting his heavy head on her lap. She stroked them both, her thoughts turning around Teagan. He'd said nothing about why Alan would think she was Abby's mother.

"Could just be a simple misunderstanding," she said to herself. But she still wanted to know. She'd let tough conversations slide for several days now, so she pulled out her phone and called Teagan.

"Hey," he said. "Did you leave something in my car?"

"No," she said. "I want to know why Alan thought I was Abby's mom." Her heart pounded in her chest, but this was important. Somehow, she needed to know.

"I don't know."

"You're not a great liar," she said, stung that he thought he could lie to her at this point in their relationship.

"I've heard that before," he said.

"Okay, then there's a reason, and you know what it is." Gwen didn't want to play games, and she didn't think Teagan wanted to either. He simply didn't want to talk about hard things at all. Ever.

But he has, she told herself in the silence following her statement. He'd talked to her about children and his daughter and his family issues. Well, some of them. He'd mentioned quite a bit about his previous relationship with Caroline Faye, and Gwen liked the man he was now.

After all, everyone had a past. Those experiences shaped a person, helped them learn what they wanted and didn't want.

He still hadn't spoken, and Gwen wanted to bail him out. But she held on and waited a moment longer. Then another moment. "You don't want to tell me," she said.

"Not right now," he said.

"All right," she said, though she wasn't sure how anything he still hadn't told her would be worse or more dangerous to their relationship than what he'd already confided. "I'll see you at dinner, then." She hung up before he could say more, and she wasn't surprised when he didn't text or call.

She'd given him an out, and he'd taken it.

Gwen felt like she'd gone backward ten steps in the span of ten minutes. And they'd barely gone forward five steps on this trip. It seemed like every step they took toward a happy and fulfilling relationship required the navigation of a pothole, some deeper than others. A few feet backward. Then forward again.

She wasn't afraid of the journey, but she did wonder if it was worth it. Would there be something worthwhile at the end of the path? Or would she end up with a broken heart all over again?

18

Teagan paced in the short hallway that led to the kitchen. Gwen wasn't in her office, and he was early to meet her at the inn for dinner. He still had no idea how to tell her that he'd once told Alan that the only woman he could see himself with was Caroline Faye.

Even after they'd broken up, he'd wanted her back. He'd returned to the Shores a couple of times, and he'd sat with Alan for a few hours during a slow time at the breakfast shop. He'd told him that he'd never be happy with anyone besides his daughter's mother.

But he hadn't met Gwen Heartwood yet, and those words had been spoken by a much younger man, who really had no idea what he was talking about.

"Seems like you do that a lot," he muttered to himself. He turned when he got to the door that led into the kitchen, and he'd only taken a couple of steps before Gwen rounded the corner.

"Oh," she said, freezing on the spot. "You're here already."

He had no idea what to say to her now, just like he hadn't earlier when she'd called. "I got here early," he said, cursing himself for not being able to be the kind of man she needed. The kind of man she wanted. The kind of man she *deserved*.

"I've been thinking a lot," Gwen said, twisting her fingers around themselves. "And it feels like we've regressed to where we were last time you broke up with me."

"No," he said, but Gwen started nodding.

"You said on the trip that you needed to see someone. I think...." She swallowed and looked away. "I think you should do that, Teagan. Take care of yourself. And then we can try again."

"I don't need to do that," he said.

She nodded. "Yeah, maybe not. You get to decide." She lifted her chin and looked him right in the eyes. Hers were so bright, and so pretty, and he felt like she was carving his heart out of his chest with every word she said. "I like this man you are now, but I don't think he's whole. And I want all of you." She fell back a step. "So I'm going to cancel dinner, and I guess I'll see you at work tomorrow morning."

"Gwen," he said, feeling every cell in his body start to

wail. "Don't do this."

"I want you, Teagan," she said. "But I want all of you. Not just the parts you feel like telling me. I want who you were twenty years ago, and who you are now. And I don't think you're ready for all of that."

He couldn't argue with her. He was ready for part of it. If he could just be who he was now, he'd be fine. But he was the culmination of all thirty-nine years of his life.

And besides, Gwen was right. She deserved all of him. *I want you, Teagan.*

"I'll see you at work," she said, and then she turned and went back the way she'd come. He stayed in the hallway, his fingers clenching and unclenching, wondering what to do now.

He couldn't stay right there in the hall, so he followed Gwen, turning left when she'd gone right. That hall took him toward the main entrance to Redfin, but he bypassed that and continued outside.

Gwen was right; the beach here felt full of energy and vibrancy, despite not having any more people than the one at the Shores.

He didn't have anywhere else to go, but at least he wouldn't run into Gwen out here. He found an empty chaise and sat down, just watching the waves until it got too dark to see them. Then he went home.

The following morning found him pushing into the kitchen from the outside entrance, the metal door slamming behind him. He hadn't had to use his key, which meant one thing: Gwen had beaten him to work. He usually arrived before her, but he hadn't fallen asleep until two-thirty, so when his alarm had gone off two hours later, the first thing he'd done was hit snooze.

The scent of her fruity, floral perfume filled the air, and he couldn't stop himself from looking over to her office. The door was open, as it usually was, and he hung his keys by the door and continued into the kitchen. He'd worked here for six months without even talking to her after their last break-up, and he could do this.

Maybe.

Last time, the break-up had been his choice, and he'd beaten himself up for it every day. But this time...*this time it's your fault too*, he told himself as he got out his knives and set everything in order.

He couldn't think about a dish for that night, and he opened the binder of what Gordon had been doing for the past ten days. The door opened, and in walked the man himself.

"Hey," Gordon said with a laugh. "How was your trip?"

"Great." Teagan grinned at Gordon and shook his hand. "How did things go here?"

"Just fine. Everything's in there."

"I'm feeling...jetlagged," he said. "Will you set the specials for this week too?"

"Jetlagged?" Gordon peered at him, suspicion and concern in his eyes. "Didn't you drive like, two hours?"

"Three," Teagan said. "I'm just tired and need a few days to get back up to speed."

"I'll set the specials," Gordon said. "Put in the order to Gwen."

"Thanks," Teagan said. "You tell me what to do, and I'll do it."

Gordon steepled his fingers and cackled as if he were an evil madman. "You might regret this."

Teagan laughed, a slip of happiness moving through him. But he knew he himself wasn't happy. It was just a feeling that would fade as quickly as it had came. No, in order for him to be truly happy—be a happy person, not just experience a few moments of happiness—he needed to do what Gwen had suggested.

He needed to see a counselor and work out his past feelings.

"Morning, Gordon," Gwen said, and Teagan jerked his attention to her. She wore her professional black slacks and a pair of flat, black sneakers. Her chef's coat was buttoned precisely, and she'd wound her hair up in her classic bun. "Hi, Teagan."

"Gwen," he said at the same time Gordon engulfed her in a hug.

"Teagan said I can play head chef for another week," Gordon said. "I'll have an order to you before I leave today."

Gwen's eyebrows went up and her gaze wandered back

to Teagan. "All right. Sounds great, Gordon. Tell me where you want me on prep."

"I like this post-vacation version of you two," he said, grinning at them, obviously not feeling any of the tension skyrocketing through Teagan. "So relaxed."

Gwen managed a giggle—the same one that made Teagan want to pull her into her office and kiss her—but Teagan just shook his head and smiled.

WHEN HE GOT OFF THAT MORNING, HE DID THE SAME THINGS he always did after work: he showered, he made lunch for himself, and he put in a load of laundry. Then he did something he hadn't done in a long, long time.

He logged onto his health insurance provider and got a referral for a mental health professional. Then, keeping his courage as close as he could, he managed to dial the number for Doctor Curtis and set up an appointment for later that week.

I want you, Teagan.

And he wanted Gwen.

But first, he had to become the man she deserved.

He went to work each morning, and the space between him and Gwen was too big for him, but it wasn't as awkward as it had been last time. He worked under Gordon and revived his drive for cooking, making next week's menu and turning in the grocery list to Gwen on Thursday morning.

And that afternoon, he showered, made himself lunch, and went to his first appointment with Doctor Curtis. He didn't quite know what to expect, but he knew he'd have to talk a lot. His nerves bounced around in his muscles and veins as he waited in the office, and when his name was called, he could hardly stand up.

But stand up he did, and he walked into the office too. A man wearing a sweater vest rose from behind a table, and Teagan stalled. "Hello," he said, surprised for some reason. "I thought...never mind."

"I was a woman." Doctor Curtis smiled and approached him. "I get that a lot. I've asked my mom a dozen times why she thought Tracy was a good name for a boy." He chuckled and stepped forward to shake Teagan's hand. "If you'd rather see a woman, I can give you a referral."

"No, I'm fine," Teagan said, some of the initial shock wearing off. "Nice to meet you. I'm Teagan Hatch."

"I've eaten at Redfin many times," Doctor Curtis said. "That's your food, right?"

"It takes a team of people to run a restaurant," he said, moving over to the couch and sitting down.

"So you're not here to learn humility," Doctor Curtis said, smiling as he sat in the recliner opposite of Teagan. "Tell me why you *are* here."

He swallowed. Took a deep breath. Gathered his

courage. And said, "I'm in love with a woman, and I need to fix some things before I try to get her back."

"Can I talk to you for a sec?" he asked Gwen later that night. They'd just finished another successful dinner service, and he was feeling more and more like his old self in the kitchen.

She looked at him, her blue eyes sharp and wary at the same time. "I suppose. In private?"

"Yes, please." He glanced down the line where Lauren was still cleaning up her station.

Gwen nodded and strode toward her office. Teagan watched her for a moment, a wave of appreciation flowing over him. Last time they'd split up, everything between them was shattered. He knew he'd caused that breakage—and this one too—but this time it wasn't as bad. He was stronger. Or Gwen was. Or something.

Maybe he just knew her better. Knew what he wanted better.

He followed her into the office but didn't close the door. "Okay, so I know I just had ten days off, but I'm going to beg for another few days."

"Oh." Gwen's eyebrows lifted. "You want time off. I wasn't expecting that."

"What were you expecting?"

"I have no idea." She sighed as she sat behind her

desk. She ran her fingers along her forehead as if she had an ache there she couldn't soothe. Teagan wanted to fix everything for her, but he couldn't do that.

Thankfully, his hour with Doctor Curtis that day had helped him see what he could fix. He cleared his throat. "I need to go to California for a quick trip."

That statement brought Gwen's eyes right back to his, questions and curiosity swimming in those ocean-colored depths now. "Oh?"

Teagan nodded and sat down, his head feeling bobbly and wobbly. "I need to talk to my daughter. I need to talk to my ex-wife. I need to find some closure there. Ask for some forgiveness." He gazed evenly at her. "I'm trying, Gwen."

He was trying, and he was so miserable at the same time. Being in this office with her felt like self-inflicted torture.

"How much time do you need?" she asked. "And when?" She opened a drawer and pulled out the long sheet of paper she used to schedule things in the kitchen.

"I can go any time," he said. "Whenever it's most convenient for you."

"Okay." She hummed as she looked at the schedule. "Celeste has the Wilder wedding coming up. I need you for that." She glanced at him. "Could you go on the fourteenth?"

Teagan swiped on his phone and started tapping to get to the calendar. "That's over two weeks away."

"We have a family reunion this week," she said. "I need you for that. And we have that swimming club coming next week, with the wedding right on top of that."

Teagan's disappointment cut through him, but he masked it as well as he could. Gwen probably saw it, but he wasn't sure. And he wasn't going to ask. "October fourteenth is fine," he said.

"And we have the Halloween carnival starting on the twenty-first. Is seven days enough time?"

Teagan sincerely hoped so, and he nodded, made a note in his calendar app, and stood up. "Yes. Thank you, Gwen." He started to leave, but she said his name, causing him to turn back. He really liked it when she said his name with so much emotion behind it. "Yeah?"

She stood up too. "I really hope you can find the closure you need in California."

He did too, and he nodded again before leaving the office. He didn't need to just go to California to make things right, but he didn't want to tell her he had to return to the Shores and face his mother.

He'd tell her after it was all said and done. When he was on her front steps, asking her to go out with him again. When he was the man she needed him to be.

19

"I feel like a complete jerk," Gwen said into her coffee mug. She didn't drink coffee in the evening, but then again, she wasn't normally home at this time of night either. Celeste's boyfriend was bringing dinner, and Gwen's stomach growled.

"Why?" her sister asked. "Because you told Teagan what you needed? Better now than after you're married, right?"

Married. Gwen wasn't sure that was going to happen for her. She hadn't been able to focus on anyone but Teagan for almost a year now, and she felt time slipping away from her.

"Right?" Celeste prompted. Her older sister could be a bit intense sometimes.

"I suppose," Gwen said as something clunked against the floor. "He has one of your shoes."

"Joey." Celeste flew from her seat at the table and toward the dog. "No. Shoes are not for dogs." She started wrestling the pale pink wedge from the mutt's mouth, finally succeeding with a huff as the doorbell rang.

Gwen should've gotten up to help her, but well, she wasn't feeling much like doing anything at the moment. Celeste sighed as she wiped her hair out of her face and looked at the door as her boyfriend entered, a couple of bags clutched in his hands.

"He did it again," Brad said. "Joey. You've got to leave her shoes alone." He closed the door, and the scent of fried chicken started to fill the house. "I'm sorry, sweetheart. I'll pay you back for those." And he could too, because he'd played professional football for seventeen years and had tons of money.

"It's fine," Celeste said, tossing the shoe toward the box where she kept the dog toys. A couple of Gwen's were in there too, but she'd willingly given them to Joey.

"It's a shoe," Celeste said. "Tell me that's from Jack-Jack's."

"It is, and I got the brown gravy and the peppered gravy." He smiled at her. "I'm really sorry about Joey. Should I take him back to the shelter?"

Gwen's heart stalled. She loved Joey, and she didn't want to get rid of him, despite the shoe-chewing. If Brad didn't want him, Gwen would take him.

"No way," Celeste said, bending to pat the mutt. "He

just needs some obedience classes. Sit. Sit." She pointed to the ground and straightened, and the dog sat. "See?"

Gwen almost scoffed, because she was the one who'd spent the last several afternoons training Joey to sit. And fetch a ball. And shake hands. She just hadn't shown Celeste all of his tricks yet.

Brad grinned and moved into the kitchen. "Let's eat. I'm starving."

"I'll bet. You started the day out in Mount Vernon Hills, right?" She followed him, giggling when he took her into his arms and kissed her.

"Gross," Gwen said, though she found Celeste and Brad's romance absolutely swoon-worthy. "If there's not a crispy chicken potato bowl in there for me, you're never allowed in this house again." She got up and put her coffee mug in the sink.

Brad stepped over to the bag and pulled out Gwen's dinner. "For you, Gwenny."

"I can't believe I let you call me that."

"You like it," Brad said. "How are things in the kitchen?"

Gwen tossed a look at Celeste, willing her to keep their secrets. Gwen had kept some for Celeste, even when it had been hard. "Hot," she finally said.

"Is that a good hot or a bad hot?" Brad watched her for a moment, and while she liked the guy, she wasn't going to spill her guts to him.

"It's just hot." She sat back down at the kitchen table and took the lid off her bowl.

"Before we eat, I have a question," Brad said. When Gwen looked up again, he'd fallen to both knees.

"Oh, my goodness," Celeste said, her words made of only air.

Pure happiness moved through Gwen. Fine, with a pinch of jealousy. "Here it comes," she said, smiling for all she was worth.

"Celeste," Brad said. "I'm in love with you. I know I've never said it out loud, but I've been feeling it more and more lately. I love you. I want to marry you in that outdoor wedding hall, and have a family with you, and take our kids to the nice beach every afternoon."

Gwen sighed, his words perfect and the scene of Celeste's wedding playing out in her mind. Celeste started weeping, her hand clutched right to her throat.

"Will you marry me?" he asked, reaching to open a drawer.

"How long has that been there?" she asked as he pulled a black velvet ring box out of the drawer where she and Gwen kept their large kitchen utensils. "You kept a diamond ring with spatulas?"

"He's asking you to marry him," Gwen said. "Stop criticizing how he's doing it." She'd put the ring there when she'd gotten home from work that morning. Brad had met her near the kitchen and told her the plan. Since Celeste didn't cook, and Brad had said he was bringing dinner, there'd be no reason for her sister to open that drawer.

"I'm not criticizing how he's doing it," Celeste said.

"You haven't answered," Brad said, drawing her attention back to him. He opened the box to show a really beautiful diamond. So maybe Gwen had looked at it for a few minutes. Or an hour. She wasn't sure.

"Yes," Celeste said, reaching to cradle his face in both of her hands. "Yes, I'll marry you."

He grinned and swooped her into his arms, laughing as he twirled her around. "Great. Is eight months long enough to plan the wedding?"

"More than enough," she said. "And I love you too, Bradley Keith." She kissed him, and since they'd just gotten engaged, Gwen couldn't tell them to stop.

She looked at her crispy chicken potato bowl and smiled, her emotions spiraling up to make her eyes wet. In the next few moments, her smile faded and Brad and Celeste joined her at the table, but she didn't want to look at them. Then they'd see how unhappy she was when she should be asking them about their wedding.

"Hey." Brad's hand came down on Gwen's, and she met his eyes. "I've been talking to you. Are you okay?" He glanced at Celeste, who thankfully said nothing.

"I'm...okay. Sorry." She shook her head. "What did you say?"

"I asked why you weren't at Redfin tonight. Don't you work there most evenings?"

"Yes," she said. "Just needed a night off."

"I haven't heard about your trip either," he said.

"Brad," Celeste said, and Gwen appreciated her sister so much right then.

"The trip was great," she said. "I learned a lot about my boyfriend, and that's why he isn't my boyfriend anymore."

"Gwenny," Brad said. "I'm sorry. I didn't know."

"I'm okay." She picked up her food and added, "I'm going to eat on the back porch so you two can talk about your wedding."

"You don't need to leave," Celeste said.

But Gwen did. She didn't run out, though. She stepped over to Celeste and gave her a hug. "I'm so happy for you." Her voice broke on the last word, and she pulled away. Brad stood up and blocked her exit, pulling her into a hug too.

He said nothing, because what could he say? He didn't know Teagan. He didn't know what had happened on the trip. He didn't have a magic wand that would allow Gwen to go back in time and erase what she'd said to Teagan.

She did want him. She wanted more time with him. She wanted to know everything about him. She wanted to grow old with him. And she wanted to have kids with him.

The dogs came with her out onto the back porch, and she sat in her usual spot on the couch. They jumped up behind her and looked at her earnestly, clearly asking her to share some of that crispy chicken with them.

"I'm in love with him," she told them. "And I don't even know how it happened." She fed them each a bite of chicken and then took a few bites herself. "And the worst part? I'm so selfish that I told him he wasn't whole, and I deserved all of him."

Tears filled her eyes then, and she made no effort to wipe them away. Maybe she wasn't whole without him. She just hadn't thought that far ahead.

She pulled in a deep breath and calmed herself enough to keep eating. Teagan was taking some time off. He was going to California. Hopefully, whatever he needed to do there could get done, and they could try again.

She didn't want to go back to the dating pool. She couldn't make it through twenty-four more dates before she found another keeper, and she'd read an article that some women went on forty-one dates before finding Mister Right.

"You've found him," she told herself and the dogs now happily licking the gravy remains from her bowl. Now she just needed to give him some time to figure out if he wanted her too.

THE DAYS PASSED, AND GWEN DIDN'T FEEL LIKE SHE NEEDED to hide from Teagan. They worked together just fine. Cooking with him had always been exciting, and that hadn't diminished. She allowed herself to feel the adventure of it, whereas last time he'd ended things with her, even seeing him made her angry.

But now, she could be in the same room with him. Talk to him. Look at him. She just had to escape to her office a couple of times and take a few deep breaths. She had to cry in the shower between her shifts. Stare longingly out at the waves during the afternoons she used to spend with him.

She was fine.

She was also lying to herself.

October fourteenth came, and Teagan didn't come into the kitchen. Everything felt vastly different without him there, and Gwen wasn't sure if the relief she felt was good or bad. Because along with it came a heavy sense that something wasn't quite right.

The Heartwood Inn needed Teagan Hatch in its kitchen. She wondered if Teagan would even come back. He hadn't quit, but he'd given her nothing after his initial request to be gone. He'd taken all seven days she could give him, and her heart started thumping in a strange way.

"I'll be right back," she managed to say to Gordon.

"We open in ten," he said, and she nodded. She knew what time it was. She knew she was on the eggs and hash browns that morning. It was the busiest station in the kitchen during their brief breakfast service, and she could do it.

What she couldn't do was continue working at the inn

without Teagan. She hurried to her office and closed the door, her breaths coming in huge gulps now.

A groan rumbled in her throat, and she bent over, bracing herself on her knees, trying to breathe.

"Please let him come back," she said, everything in her blitzing with pain and light. "Please let him come back."

20

Teagan got off the plane in Los Angeles, a swarm of angry bees stinging his stomach. But there was no turning back now. Doctor Curtis had encouraged him to find any open doors that needed to be closed, and close them.

And the one with Caroline and Abby was wide open. He wanted to keep the door open with Abby, but in order to move on with another woman, he needed to speak to both of them. Surprisingly, Caroline had answered his texts easily, and she'd arranged for a driver to pick him up at the airport.

He passed the security line of people going in, glad he didn't have to wait for his luggage. A stuffy man wearing a black suit and sunglasses held a placard with his first and last name on it, and Teagan lifted his hand and said, "I'm Teagan Hatch."

"ID please," he said, and Teagan sighed inwardly. Caroline had said she had quite the security detail, and Teagan supposed that was smart. He dug in his back pocket for his wallet and produced his ID.

The man studied it as if his glasses were equipped with scanners and computers that could verify Teagan's ID. Maybe they were. "Right this way," he finally said, leading Teagan toward the exit.

A sleek, black car waited in the first lane, only steps through the door. The security guard opened the back door and Teagan ducked inside.

"Hello, Teagan," Caroline said, startling him.

"Caroline." He wasn't expecting her to be in the car. "You didn't have to come. I thought we were meeting later."

"I'm not filming today," she said as the door closed behind him. The guard got in the front seat, not that Teagan could see or hear him. But the car shifted with his weight, and then it eased away from the curb.

"I haven't heard from you in years," she said, obviously wanting him to say why he needed to see her so urgently. Not that he'd flown out the moment he wanted to. He couldn't leave the kitchen at Heartwood for days and days.

"I know," he said. "I just...I needed to see you." He barely glanced at her though. "How's Abby?" The question just slipped between his lips. He wasn't even sure why he'd asked.

Caroline leveled her gaze at him and slowly reached

for a pair of sunglasses perched on the armrest beside her. She slid them on, concealing her eyes from him. "You would know better than me, Teagan."

"Really?"

"She hasn't spoken to me in a while." Caroline sounded calm and collected and as if their daughter's silence didn't bother her in the slightest.

But alarm moved through Teagan. "What happened?"

"Does this have any bearing on why you needed to talk to me?" she asked. "Why you flew all the way across the country when I haven't heard from you or seen you in over eight years?"

Frustration built in Teagan. "I think it might, yeah." He looked away from her, not really caring where this car was taking him. He'd told Caroline where he was staying while he was in the city, and they'd planned to meet at the on-site restaurant later that night.

"I need to know you got the money I sent all those years."

"I did."

And yet, she'd said nothing. "I'm sure you didn't need it, but it was important to me that I send it."

Caroline said nothing, and he hated how perfectly still she sat, as if she were some sort of china doll.

"I need to tell you that I didn't mean to hurt you or Abby." He'd already expressed his anger and displeasure with Caroline and her decision not to tell him about the pregnancy and birth of his daughter.

"We know that," Caroline said.

"I've met someone else," Teagan said. "And I just want to make sure I can stick around for her. I'm just...never been good at being a boyfriend, husband, or father."

Several seconds of silence passed before Caroline reached over and covered Teagan's hand with hers. "You did just fine, Teagan. I fell madly in love with you, because you were the best boyfriend I'd ever had."

"Yeah, but that wasn't hard," he said. "You'd only dated losers before me."

"And losers since," she said, squeezing his hand. "We simply weren't meant to be. Our split was as much my fault as yours. Probably more. And I bear the burden of concealing Abby from you for years. So I'm not quite sure why you think you can't be a good boyfriend or husband."

So many things stormed within Teagan. "I'm not sure why either," he said. "Only that I've never felt good enough."

"Well, I am an international superstar," Caroline said with a lilting tease in her voice. "Is your new girlfriend an actress?"

"No." Thank goodness.

"A singer? Country music star, perhaps? You are still in the South, aren't you?"

"Yes," he said. "But she's not a country music star. She's a chef at the inn where I work."

"Ah, a soulmate, then."

Teagan swung his attention to his ex-wife, finding a soft smile on her face. "You don't even know her."

"But I know you, Teagan."

"You did, once," he said. "A long time ago." She didn't know him now, which only made his desperate need to make sure everything was right between them all the more insane.

"I know you love cooking," she said. "You always have. Remember how we met?"

Teagan remembered. "You were starving on-set and wouldn't eat the snacks they'd brought in. So I gathered a bunch of stuff and took it to your trailer, where I made you an amazing sandwich." He had always loved putting together sandwiches.

Caroline gave a delicate laugh, sobering quickly as the car slowed to a stop. Something beeped, and then a man said, "We're at the hotel, ma'am."

She removed her hand from Teagan's. "We don't need to meet tonight, Teagan. You and I? We're good. The only thing I wish was that I hadn't been so stupid and let you walk out of my life." Her smile turned sad, and she looked out her window. "Your girlfriend is very lucky, and I hope you find a way to make things work with her."

Teagan hadn't spoken to Caroline in a long time, but he knew finality when he heard it. And she was done talking.

"Thank you, Caroline," he said, reaching for the door handle. He opened the door to find the security guard there. He nodded to the man and walked away from the car, his head held high. As he entered the hotel, a sense of cleansing filled him.

He'd told Alan many years ago that if he ever started dating and got married again, it would only be to his daughter's mother.

But he'd never reached out to Caroline. Never wanted to put himself back in her life.

And now he knew why—a relationship never would've worked between them, for one. And for a second, she wasn't Gwen Heartwood.

He fumbled in his pocket for his phone, dialing Gwen faster than he ever had before. Her line rang and rang, and she didn't pick up before it went to voicemail.

His heart raced as he oscillated between leaving a message and simply hanging up. What would he even say?

I love you, Gwen.

Yeah, he couldn't say that in a voicemail message. The beep sounded before he hung up, so he said, "Hey, Gwen. I have something to tell you. Call me when you get a chance, okay?" He wasn't sure if she would, but he'd try her later, when it wasn't naptime on the East Coast and he wasn't standing in a lobby filled with people.

He waited his turn to check in, surprised by the number of people there that afternoon. He learned there was a conference at the hotel, and everything made sense. Finally up in his room, he texted Abby.

I'm in town. Landed a couple of hours ago. Want to get dinner tonight?

His daughter started typing, at least according to his phone. *I thought you were meeting Mom tonight.*

She picked me up at the airport. I'm free tonight if you are.

I am...if you're willing to meet my boyfriend.

"Boyfriend," Teagan muttered, already disliking the guy. *Sure*, he typed out instead. *I'd love to meet him.*

Great, she said. *I'll text you a great place we can meet. Okay?*

"Okay," he said out loud as he typed it. She didn't respond right away, but Teagan wasn't worried.

Abby talked to him and not Caroline. He wondered why, and he needed to know what had happened between them.

He needed to know how Abby felt about him as a father, and he needed Gwen to call him back. Sitting down on the bed, he tried doing the meditation Doctor Curtis had taught him, only to have his calm, restful state broken by the ringing of his phone only ten minutes later.

Didn't matter.

Gwen's name sat on the screen.

"Hey," he said easily, though every cell in his body was now firing at maximum capacity.

"You wanted me to call?" she said, bypassing the fun, flirty greetings she usually gave him.

"Yes," he said, clearing his throat. "I once told Alan that if I ever dated or got married again, it would be to my daughter's mother. That's why he thought you were Caroline."

A very pregnant pause came through the line. Then Gwen said, "Oh."

"I'm in California," he said. "And I've seen Caroline." He had no idea how to say what he felt. "And she's not the one for me, so what I said all those years ago is just more proof of how stupid I was."

"I see."

"We all say stupid things sometimes," he said. "Right?"

"I just called Steven by your name about ten times," Gwen said with a sigh. "So yeah, we all say stupid things sometimes."

He chuckled, though calling someone by the wrong name wasn't the same as making definitive life statements about how things would be.

"I'm meeting Abby and her boyfriend for dinner," he said, so glad he was able to talk to Gwen about this.

"That sounds fun," she said, a false note in her voice.

"Yeah." Teagan stood up and paced to the windows, working up the courage to say what he wanted to. "I wish you were here," he finally said.

Gwen's voice was very low when she said, "I hope you find what you need in California." She had to go a moment later, and the call ended.

Teagan looked out the window at the sprawling city before him. He really disliked the city, even if it did have water on the west border. He'd grown up with sand in his hair and the sound of the surf in his ears. He loved islands and oceans and beaches.

And he loved Gwen Heartwood.

Don't let her get away, he told himself.

Make things work, Caroline had said.

He could only imagine what Abby would say, and he couldn't wait for their dinner that night.

He stepped off the elevator and adjusted the jacket he wore. Abby had texted him to meet her and Scott at a "semi-upscale" restaurant a few blocks from his hotel, and he didn't want to be late. He made the short walk quickly, entering the restaurant a few minutes early only to find Abby sitting beside a handsome man.

She laughed at something he said, and with the two of them smiling like that, Teagan could sense their happiness way down in his toes. It was the kind of happiness he wanted for her—and for himself. It was the kind of happiness that filled a person and lasted. Not a fleeting moment of something good happening, but true happiness.

"Abby," he said, drawing her attention. He couldn't believe he was nervous to see her, but he was. The last time had been a few years ago, when she'd graduated from high school. He'd flown out for one day, and he hadn't spoken to Caroline at all.

She turned toward him, and she was beautiful and

radiant. "Dad." Abby jumped to her feet and threw herself into his arms.

Teagan held on, because such fierce feelings of love moved through him for this human he'd helped create. "Oh, it's so good to see you," he said. "And not just in pictures."

Abby held him tightly too as her boyfriend stood. Teagan just smiled at him and waited until Abby stepped back. She wiped at her eyes quickly and backed up to her boyfriend's side. "Dad, this is my boyfriend, Scott Arrow. Scott, my dad, Teagan Hatch."

"It's so great to meet you," Scott said, extending his hand for Teagan to shake. He had a good air about him, and it was obvious he adored Abby.

"And you," Teagan said. They shook hands, and a sense of awkwardness descended on Teagan. "How long have you guys been dating?"

"A while," Scott said at the same time Abby said, "Eight months."

"Eight months?" Teagan's eyebrows went up. "You never said anything." And what about that cute guy she'd been talking to only a month ago?

"You'd just broken up with Gwen," Abby said. "I didn't want to upset you."

"Abby." Teagan sighed and looked away, feeling like a failure. "I want you to be happy. You having a boyfriend wouldn't upset me." His brain whirred. "And how did you know about me and Gwen?" Had he even told her Gwen's name?

"I just knew," she said. "Even from across the country, Dad, you have a way of broadcasting your emotions." She grinned at him and led them over to the hostess stand. "We're all here now."

She grabbed three menus and led them to a table. Abby and Scott were very cute together, Teagan could admit that. "She'll want a picture of you two," he said. "Lean in close together."

Abby and Scott complied, and Teagan took a picture with his phone.

"I thought you two broke up," Abby said, reaching for her water glass.

"I'm trying to get her back," Teagan said. "And she's my boss, so I still talk to her."

"And that's why you wanted to meet with Mom," Abby said, her voice notably cooler.

"Yeah." He looked up from his phone. "And you. I wanted to apologize for not being the greatest father on the planet."

"Dad." She reached across the table and touched his hand. "We've talked about this. You were fine."

"Why don't you talk to your mother?"

"Why don't you?" She glanced at Scott, but he wisely said nothing. When she looked back at Teagan, she wore a challenge in her eyes.

"She's...difficult," Teagan said. "I don't have to talk to her. But she's your mom."

"She didn't raise me," Abby said. "Cindi did, using the money you sent."

Teagan cocked his head at her. "What? Caroline has lots of money."

"Yeah, I know." Abby sighed. "She paid for the house and stuff, but Cindi would use your money to pay for my clothes, my lunch money, all of it."

Teagan had no idea what to say. Caroline Faye had been in dozens of movies. She could certainly pay for her daughter's clothes. Couldn't she?

"Dad, I don't talk to her, because she doesn't care about me," Abby said. "And you do."

"How do you know that?" he asked.

"Because you text and call. You send me grocery money out of the blue just because you want me to be able to eat more than canned soup. You always call on my birthday, and you ask me about my classes and work and swimming."

"I didn't know about Scott."

"Mom doesn't either. And she doesn't ask. Doesn't send anything. Never calls. She doesn't care about me."

"I'm sure—"

"She didn't come to my graduation. She doesn't know where I live. She has no idea what I'm studying in school." Abby glared now. "So don't tell me you're sure she does. Actions speak louder than words, Dad."

"She didn't come to your graduation?"

"Cindi did. Cindi helped me pack my stuff and move into a student apartment. Cindi calls and texts and sends cards on my birthday."

Teagan couldn't believe what she was saying. "I'm so sorry, Abby. I didn't know." He would've done more. Maybe moved here to be closer to her so she didn't feel so isolated.

"It's fine," she said. "But whatever you're beating yourself up about, you should stop. You're a great dad, and I love you."

"I love you too, bug," he said, sudden emotion choking him.

"All right." Abby shook out her dark hair, so much like Caroline's. "So let's start strategizing about how you can get Gwen back."

21

Just ask O for a room.

Gwen read Celeste's text and wondered if she really could just stay at the inn for a couple of nights. She wasn't sure why, but she didn't want to be in the house alone, and Celeste was off the island on a business trip.

Okay, she sent to Celeste, immediately starting a text to Olympia too. Twenty minutes later, she picked up a keycard from Nancy at the front desk and headed to one of the eighteenth floor corner suites.

Teagan was supposed to be back to work tomorrow morning, and the last seven days without him in the kitchen had been torture. He had texted and they'd talked the first day. He'd even sent a picture of his daughter and her boyfriend.

But she hadn't heard from him since.

He didn't have to report to her, a fact she recited to herself as she showered and got in bed for the night. She tossed and turned, waking often to check to make sure she hadn't slept through her alarm.

Finally, she got up before it went off, got dressed in the same clothes she'd worn yesterday, and went downstairs to the kitchen. Her nerves assaulted her as she unlocked the back door, anticipating Teagan's arrival any minute.

He didn't come in, though. Gordon did. Steven did. Gage did. Harriett came to check on their bakery items. Their fresh fish was delivered. And still Teagan didn't show up.

He hadn't texted either, and a quiet desperation built beneath Gwen's tongue. She sent him a quick message —*Where are you?*—and went to see where Gordon would have her work that morning.

No one else in the kitchen seemed to be expecting Teagan. No one asked where he was, and Gordon went through the head chef duties, as he'd been doing for the past week already.

Just as breakfast service was about to start, Harriett's voice crackled on the radio. "Gwen, I need you up in the bakery immediately."

She looked at Gordon, who said, "Go, we're fine here."

Gwen took off her apron, though it was still pristine, and headed toward the door that would take her behind the bakery counter. It had been open for hours, but their hot service hadn't quite started yet.

She'd only taken one step through the door when she realized there was something afoot in the bakery.

"He's refusing to leave," Harriett said, though she wore a smile and could barely deliver her sentence without giggling.

Teagan stood in the middle of the bakery, at least two dozen balloons clutched in one fist. Their colorful ties kept the balloons from floating up to the ceiling, and he looked at someone on his right.

Gwen couldn't look away from him, even when everyone in the bakery started singing. A few seconds passed before the song registered in her ears and mind. They were singing *Happy Birthday*, but it wasn't her birthday.

They finished with a rousing cheer, the entire kitchen staff crowding into the space behind her, pushing her forward and around the bakery cases holding their breads, muffins, and doughnuts.

"What's going on?" she asked as the applause died down. She still stood a healthy distance from Teagan, because she didn't trust herself not to kiss him in front of all these people.

"It's my birthday," he said, his smile never wavering. "And I only want one thing."

Gwen's pulse zoomed and zinged around in her veins

as he stepped forward. "And that's you, Gwen Heartwood. I know I'm not perfect. I know I'm not quite the man you deserve. But I'm in love with you, and I think if you gave me a third chance, we'd be able to...."

Panic crossed his face and he looked at pretty young woman with dark hair. "Be able to have an amazing life together," she said in a *very* loud stage whisper. Several people in the bakery—strangers!—twittered, and Gwen had no idea what was going on.

"Right." Teagan looked at Gwen again. "I think if you gave me a third chance, we'd be able to have an amazing life together."

Gwen wanted to give him all the chances he needed. Because she loved him too.

"I'm sorry I couldn't tell you everything at the Shores," he said. "But I have now, and I'm committed to telling you anything else you want to know, when you want to know it." He glanced at the woman again, and everything fell into place.

She realized who she was at the same time Teagan said, "This is my daughter, Abby. She wanted to meet you, and I know you wanted to meet her."

Gwen stared at the woman, pure wonder filling her. She took a few steps and grabbed onto Abby, hugging her tight. "You helped him with this, didn't you?"

"Oh, my dad is hopeless with stuff like this," she whispered back. "And hopelessly in love with you." She pulled back, tears in her eyes even as she grinned at Gwen. "Maybe put him out of his misery?"

They both looked at Teagan, who wore such a hopeful expression on his face. Gwen decided she didn't care that there were strangers watching. Her entire kitchen staff. His daughter.

She was going to kiss him in front of everyone.

With her shoulders squared, she looked right at him. "I'm in love with you, too, Teagan. If you really want me, I'm yours."

The crowd cheered, and Teagan let go of all the balloons to take her into his arms and kiss her. Gwen laughed as she tried to kiss him back, so much love and joy flowing through her. She finally sobered enough to kiss him properly, so happy in that moment that she hoped it would never end.

But end it did, and Teagan laced his fingers through hers. "I'm having breakfast sent out to the beach," he said. "Let's go. I have so much to tell you."

They left the bakery, which seemed to back to its normal operations before they'd even stepped out of the door. "What about the breakfast service?" she asked.

"Gordon's got it covered."

"Your daughter?"

"She came with her boyfriend. They have plenty to keep them occupied."

Without another reason to hang back, Gwen finally just accepted that she'd be eating breakfast on the beach with Teagan. He said, "After I went to California, I went back to the Shores," before they'd even sat down.

He'd booked one of their cabanas, and none other than Gage, her sister's boyfriend, appeared to serve them cream cheese croissants and orange juice.

"I had to see my mother again," Teagan said as he poured their juice. Gordon himself set down a platter of bacon and sausage links, squeezed Gwen's shoulder, and left. Everything was happening so fast, and she just sat and waited while Steven appeared with pancakes and syrup.

Teagan was very good, she'd give him that. When had Gordon and Steven even had time to make this food?

"And I found some closure with the things I'd been stewing over," he said. "With my ex-wife. With my daughter. With my childhood. With my mother."

"Wow." Gwen took a sip of her juice. Maybe the sugar would jumpstart her brain. "That's a lot of closure."

"I have the people in my life I need and want," he said. "And that doesn't include Caroline or my mom anymore. It is what it is."

"You're not going to talk to your mother?"

"Yes, I'll talk to her," he said. "But she doesn't get to influence how I feel anymore."

"What happened with her?"

"I said a lot of things that needed to be said. She apologized. Said she'd try not to make suggestions about my life I didn't need." He picked up a piece of bacon. "It went better than I thought it would, actually."

Gwen marveled at this man in front of her. He seemed identical to the Teagan she knew...but different too. Better. Happier.

"I'm seeing a counselor," he said. "I'm going to keep doing that for a while. I'm not in a rush to get married and have kids. Are you?"

Gwen choked on her bite of pancake, swallowing it a bit too quickly. After washing everything down with another gulp of orange juice, she shook her head. "I'm only thirty. I have time to get married and have kids."

Teagan grinned at her and leaned over to kiss her. He was sweet and gentle, and Gwen felt loved by him. "Okay," he said. "Thank you for being patient with me."

Gwen kept her eyes closed and leaned her forehead against his. "Thank you for coming back," she whispered, sending the same gratitude toward heaven.

Six months later:

"It's not going to be warm there," Teagan said from the doorway of Gwen's bedroom.

She turned, a bikini still clutched in her fingers. "So you're saying I don't need this."

"The ocean isn't warm there like it is here," he said.

"Not until August or September, at least." He eyed the swimwear. "But I'd like to see you wearing that."

Gwen hid the strappy swimming suit behind her back. "We'll have to go to the Shores again."

"Done," he said, finally entering her room. "Are you excited for our second trip together?"

"Yes," she said honestly. "I've never been to California, and I can't wait to see Abby again." His daughter had come to South Carolina for both Thanksgiving and Christmas, but it was her turn to shine on the California coast as she was graduating from college in just a few days.

"She loves you," Teagan said, wrapping his arms around her from behind. "I'm so glad you like her, Gwenny."

"I love her," Gwen said. "I mean, I know she's not my daughter, but it sort of feels like she is."

"And the age difference isn't weird?"

She'd told him half a dozen times that it wasn't. Abby had too, more than that. "No," she said. "Will Caroline be there?"

"I told Abby she should invite her, but I'm not sure she did."

His daughter had turned twenty-one in December, and Gwen thought Teagan did a great job of parenting an adult child. She wasn't that much older than twenty-one, and she knew she liked making her own decisions at that age. Sure, she'd listen to her parents, but she didn't always do what they said. Teagan didn't take offense to it when Abby did the same thing, and Gwen liked that.

"Hey, before we go," he said, turning her in his arms so they faced one another. "My daughter is wearing a diamond ring, and I was thinking it might be a nice surprise if you showed up with one too."

Before Gwen could even move, he'd dropped to both knees, an engagement ring suddenly pinched in his fingers. "I feel *whole* with you, Gwen Heartwood. Utterly and completely whole, and I want to spend the rest of my life with you as my wife. Will you marry me?"

"Yes," Gwen said instantly, before her emotions could swirl and swell and choke her. Before she started crying and asking him where he'd gotten that ring, the way her sister had done. "Yes, I'll marry you."

He beamed up at her, put the ring on her finger, and then swept her into his arms. "I love you so much," he whispered just before kissing her.

And while Gwen had had moments of *she loves him, she loves him not*, in this one, there was no doubt that she loved him.

Utterly and completely.

She kissed him back, half-crying as she did so. "Will you marry me on the beach?" she asked.

"Wherever you want, Gwenny," he said. "Wherever you want."

"I want the beach," she said. "A warm beach. *Our* beach, at Heartwood."

"Done," he said, and Gwen knew when he said that, whatever he'd just agreed to would indeed be done.

"I love you," she said.

"I love you, too." Teagan kissed her again, and Gwen could not wait to become his wife.

Read on for a sneak peek at THE DAY HE DROVE BY, your next great small-town beach romance.

SNEAK PEEK! THE DAY HE DROVE BY
CHAPTER ONE

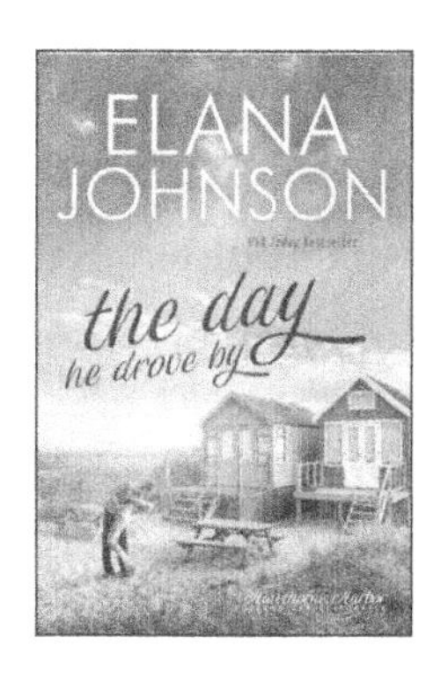

TEN YEARS AGO:

"Aaron, you have to stop the car. We're not going to make it." Gretchen Samuels hated the weakness and panic in her voice, but the pain ripping through her lower back made it difficult to speak any other way.

"We're in the middle of nowhere," her husband said. "I can't stop." In fact, he accelerated to a speed their twelve-year-old sedan certainly couldn't handle.

As another labor pain tore through her, tears spilled from Gretchen's eyes. She didn't want to have her first child on the side of the road, miles from nurses and antiseptic and baby warmers. And medication. She really needed a fast-acting painkiller.

"I'm sorry," she sobbed. Aaron hated living out on her granddad's lavender farm, but the housing was cheap and he was almost done with his online securities degree. Their plans for a future in Seattle while he led the data security team at a top technology firm were months from coming to fruition.

"Don't be sorry." He glanced at her, and she disliked the panic in his eyes too, and the white-knuckle grip he had on the steering wheel certainly wasn't comforting.

Her breath caught in her throat as it seemed like this baby was going to claw its way out of her no matter how much she willed the little girl to hold on a little longer.

"Call 911," she said. "Please." She must've infused the right amount of emotion into her voice, because Aaron slowed the car and eased it onto the gravel shoulder. He leapt from behind the wheel, left his door open, and sprinted around the front of the car.

"Let's get you into the back." He supported her—the way he'd been doing for the four years they'd been together—and helped her into the backseat before pulling out his phone and making the emergency call.

Gretchen's pain eased with the new position, but it didn't go away. She wondered if it ever would, or if this degree of agony would hover in her muscles like a ghost forever. "Hang on," she whispered as she put her hand on her very pregnant belly. "Just a little while longer."

"They're on their way." Aaron poked his head back inside the car. "They said to get any blankets, towels, napkins, anything we have. You're supposed to stay lying down and try to relax."

Gretchen couldn't help the snort that escaped. "Relax?" She let her head fall back as she focused on the car's ceiling. She hadn't been able to relax for months, not since her stomach had grown so large she couldn't see her toes. Simply getting up from the couch had grown increasingly difficult as the days had passed.

She hadn't minded, because she and Aaron had wanted this baby more than anything. The tears that heated her eyes this time were from desperation. A shiver ran over her body as the wind snaked its way into the car.

"Aaron, can you close the doors?" She lifted her head but couldn't see him anywhere. Fear flowed through her. "Aaron?"

The trunk slammed, and he came to the door closest to her head this time. "We don't have a blanket in the trunk. I found this jacket though." He balled it up and put it under her head before shrugging out of the one he was wearing too.

Gretchen steeled herself to deliver her baby and wrap it in her husband's polar fleece. Her range of emotions felt ridiculous as a wave of injustice slammed into her. "Close the doors, please," she said through tight teeth. "I'm cold." Should she be cold? What if she was going into shock or something?

Her jaw worked against the rising terror as he complied, going around the car—which had all four doors open—and shutting the wind out before sealing himself behind the wheel again. Gretchen thought the silence in the car might be worse than the wind, and she didn't want to bring her baby into the world under such a cloud of awkwardness.

"Remember when we first met?" she asked him, glad when his low, soft chuckle met her ears.

"You said my hair looked like a gorilla."

She giggled too, though the motion made her stomach muscles tighten uncomfortably. She hitched in a breath and held it. Aaron had been a freshman on campus though he was twenty-three years old. Gretchen had just finished her business management degree. His dark hair was swooped to the side, very much like the cartoon gorillas Gretchen had spent a lot of time watching while she nannied to pay for school.

He reached back and threaded his fingers through hers. "What if they don't make it?" he asked, his voice barely higher than a whisper. "I don't know how to deliver a baby."

And Gretchen knew there was more than just a baby that needed to come out. "They'll make it." She spoke with as much confidence as she could, the way she always did when Aaron confessed his worries to her.

You're the best in your class, she'd tell him. *You'll be able to find a good job.*

Don't worry about anything here, she said to him when he had to go to Seattle to take his tests, attend interviews, or deliver dissertations. *I'll be fine. Just watching the lavender grow.*

She closed her eyes and imagined herself in the fields of lavender now, the fragrant scent of the herbs wafting through the slow, blue sky. The same smile that had always accompanied her assurances when he left drifted across her face now.

Her next labor pain stole all the peace from her, and her eyes shot open and a moan ground through her whole body. Aaron's fingers on hers squeezed, and everything seemed clenched so tight, tight, tight.

The contraction seemed to last a long time before subsiding. Gretchen only got what felt like a moment's reprieve before the next one began. Time marched on, seemingly unaware of the pain she was in, the desperate way she cinched everything tight to keep the baby inside.

She wasn't sure how many labor pains she'd endured, or how much time had gone by, before Aaron said, "They're here," with a heavy dose of relief in his voice. He once again jumped from the car.

Moments later, the door by her feet opened and a gust of ocean air raced in. The scent of brine she normally loved only reminded her that this wasn't a hospital, there were no drugs, and she could do absolutely nothing about it.

"Ma'am, my name is Andrew Herrin, and I'm going to take good care of you."

She managed to look over her belly to a man who

couldn't be older than twenty. A zing of alarm raced through her.

"Drew?" She couldn't believe she cared if the man whose family lived next door to her—who she'd walked with in lavender fields as a teen—delivered her baby. He had a bag of medical supplies. A faster ride to the hospital. And a kind face, with a calm smile.

"You're going to be fine, Gretchen." He snapped a pair of gloves on and touched her ankle. "So let's see what we've got."

SNEAK PEEK! THE DAY HE DROVE BY
CHAPTER TWO

Drew Herrin felt the morning sun warm his back as he worked. He'd already fed the chickens, the horses, the cows, and the goats. His mother and stepfather had quite the little farm just north of Hawthorne Harbor, down the Lavender Highway. He glanced up and took a moment to just breathe, something he hadn't been able to do in Medina, though the town sat right on the water too.

The air simply tasted different here, and while Drew had hoped to make something of himself in Medina—do more, be better, actually help someone—he'd only realized the job was the same there as it was here. Just more stressful. Less fun. No room to run with his German shepherds and experiment with his ice cream flavors.

The wind picked up, but Drew was used to being windblown. Everyone on Hawthorne Harbor was. The long-time joke was that if you didn't like the wind, you should leave. Because it was always windy.

He looked across the water to the body of land he could just make out in the distance. He'd grown up on the harbor, but it still gave him a snip of surprise to remember he was looking at another country when he looked at that land.

For a fleeting moment, the same restlessness that had driven him to Medina three years ago squirreled through him again.

Then he put his head down and got back to work. He finished fixing the tractor his step-dad used to get the lavender fields properly built up for watering. He sharpened a few tools and whistled for his shepherds to come with him as he headed back to the house.

With a single bark, Blue announced his arrival from the huge flower garden adjacent to the farm. He brought the scent of roses with him, and even a white petal from a flower Drew would never know.

"You rascal." Drew grinned at the dog and flicked the petal to the ground. "You can't go over there." He glanced at the expansive garden, bearing row after row of flowers in all colors, shapes, and sizes. His family owned the land, but he'd learned that his mother rented it to a local florist in town, who apparently hand-grew everything she sold in her shop on Main Street.

Drew had never met the woman. She tended to the flowers when he wasn't there, obviously. And he had no need for flowers, as he'd sworn off women and all common dating practices when his last girlfriend had carved out his heart and then left town.

A text. That was what he'd gotten after a fifteen-month relationship where diamonds and children had been discussed.

I can't do this.

Drew thought the words his ex had sent now, though he tried to stuff all memories with Yvonne in them back into the box where he kept them.

Can't hadn't been in Drew's vocabulary growing up. His father had taught him to fix cars, tractors, lawn mowers, all of it. He worked the farm, rode horses, raised goats, planted lavender, and played a major role in the Hawthorne Harbor Lavender Festival. There was nothing Drew couldn't do.

He'd taken that attitude into adulthood, first finishing his emergency medical technician training and then going on to be a certified firefighter. He'd gone on to take cardiac life support classes, pediatric training, and tactical emergency care.

No, *can't* didn't exist in Drew's world. At least until Yvonne.

Something wet met his palm, and Drew danced away from his second German shepherd, the much more silent and sneaky Chief. A chuckle came from his throat, and Drew crouched to let his dogs lick his neck and face. His laughter grew, and he was reminded why this remote farm on the edge of Hawthorne Harbor felt more like home than anywhere else.

"Morning chores are done," he announced as he entered the wide, white farmhouse, his dogs right behind him. Their claws scratched against the hardwood, and he pointed to the utility room where he kept their food and water. "Go on, guys. I'll come let you out in a minute."

"Thanks, Drew," Joel said. His step-dad didn't mind the farm and the equipment upkeep, but his true love was with the lavender, and Drew figured they could both do what they liked best if he came out and tended to the animals.

Joel had spent the first thirty years of his life in trade carpentry, and he'd improved the inside and outside of the farmhouse until Drew barely recognized it. He stepped into the kitchen with the high, honey-colored wood beams slanting up to the vaulted ceiling to find his dark-haired mother standing at the stove.

"Morning, Ma." He swept a kiss along her hairline as she scrambled eggs. The smell made his stomach turn, and he opted for turning away and pouring himself a glass of orange juice. Funny how his father had passed nine years ago, and Drew still couldn't handle the sight and smell of his dad's favorite breakfast. How his mother continued making it every morning was a mystery to him. Thankfully, the grief that hit at unexpected times only tapped his heart today. Sometimes it could punch, leaving him breathless and confused.

"Are you working today?" she asked, switching her attention to a pan of sizzling bacon.

"Yep. Gonna shower and head in." He wondered what today would bring behind the wheel of the ambulance. Probably another cat stuck in another tree. Or a kid with a scrape or two. Drew chastised himself that he shouldn't *want* anyone in Hawthorne Harbor to need emergency medical care. But that seething need to *do something worthwhile* wouldn't seem to quiet today.

"Can I leave Blue and Chief here?"

"Yeah." Joel exhaled as he stood and refilled his coffee. "I'll take 'em out to the lavender fields and then let them swim in the harbor."

Drew smiled at the man. "Thanks, Joel. I promise I'll come get them tonight. The raccoons out here get them barking at night."

"Maybe they'll finally scare them away from my chickens," he said with a grumbly note in his voice. Joel certainly did love his fresh eggs and those clucky chickens.

"Breakfast?" his mother asked when Drew attempted to leave the kitchen.

"I'll stop at Duality on the way in." Part gas station and part eatery, the chefs at Duality made the best breakfast burritos Drew had ever tasted. He softened his rejection of her food with the biggest smile he could pull off and hooked his thumb over his shoulder. "I'm going to use the bathroom upstairs. I'll hang up my towel."

She didn't protest, and Drew took the steps two at a time to the mostly unused second floor. His old bedroom was up here, completely redone with the same luxurious hardwood Joel had gotten for next to nothing when a client decided they wanted something different. He'd painted the room in a light blue-gray and wispy white curtains had been added.

But the bedspread his mother had quilted still draped the bed, and Drew took a moment to run his fingertips along it. His favorite colors were green and blue, and he loved everything about being outside. So she'd carefully pieced together pine green pieces to make trees, dark brown pieces to make mountains, and several shades of blue to make the sky and ocean that surrounded this town Drew loved.

How he'd thought he could ever leave it and be happy plagued him. "Doesn't matter," he muttered to himself. He was back now, and happy helping around the farm as his parents got older, happy to have his old job back at the emergency services company that contracted with the hospital in Hawthorne Harbor, nearby Olympic National Park, and four other towns in the surrounding area.

After he showered, dressed, and let his dogs back outside, he climbed behind the wheel of his truck for the fifteen-minute drive into town. He loved the commute from farm to civilization. Though he didn't make it every day, the straight road and country stillness allowed his mind to wander along new flavor combinations for his ice cream fetish.

He'd been circling something new for a few days now, something he hadn't quite been able to put his taste buds on. He'd tried lavender and honey—that combination was as old as the Lavender Festival in town. White chocolate and lavender had been well-received among his paramedic teams, but he didn't think it special enough to enter the Festival's contest.

No, he definitely needed something special, something with that added oomph to make the Festival judges give him the coveted Lavender King title this year. He knew Augustus Hammond would enter the competition, and he'd won with ice cream three times out of the last six years. If Drew was going to take on the three-time Lavender King, it wasn't going to be with lavender and honey.

And he wasn't just competing against other food artisans. Oh, no. The town hosted the largest lavender festival in the entire country, and they gave out awards for revolutionary and best-use way of utilizing the plant that brought a new twist to old lavender traditions. He needed something special, but so far, it had eluded him.

He'd nearly arrived at the flavor that seemed to skip in and out of his mind when he saw a big, brown van on the side of the road up ahead. The vehicle looked older than him, and it sunk low on one corner, indicating a flat tire.

A blonde girl stood in the middle of the road, waving

both of her arms. Drew immediately slowed and pulled to the gravel shoulder, giving plenty of distance between his truck and the van.

"Thank goodness." The girl ran up to his truck before he could get fully out. She looked to be ten or eleven, with big front teeth she hadn't quite grown into yet. She had dark green eyes that had probably come half from her mother and half from her father. "You're the first car that's come along in an hour."

"Not much going on out here in the mornings," he said, glancing past her to the front driver's side, where the van leaned.

"My mom blew her tire, and we need help." The girl sized him up as if she could tell by looking alone if he could help or not. "Can you change a tire?"

"Sure I can." He gave her a smile, noting that all the windows on the van were glazed dark. His defenses went up, especially because her "mom" still hadn't made an appearance. Crime was low in Hawthorne Harbor—one reason he hadn't gone to the police academy to make his certifications a trifecta in public service.

But still. This non-moving van, with all those black windows, and a little girl in the middle of the road... Drew proceeded with caution.

She played with the end of her pale ponytail. "My mom will try to tell you she can do it herself." Her voice pitched lower with every word and her eyes rounded. "But don't believe her. We've been out here for over an hour, and she's cried twice. 'The flowers,' she keeps saying." The girl turned and skipped toward the van. "Come on."

Drew took out his phone and tapped out a message to his boss. *On my way in, I ran across a motorist on the side of the road. Flat tire. Just north of mile marker seventeen on the Lavender Highway. Going to check it out.*

That way, if something happened, someone knew where he was. He'd been on the Lavender Highway hundreds of times, and he'd only stopped once—to deliver a baby almost ten years ago.

He glanced around. It had been right around here too, closer to the farm than the town, out in the middle of nowhere. He wondered what had happened to Aaron and Gretchen Samuels, and the baby girl he'd wrapped in a towel before delivering the afterbirth.

Let us know if you need help came back, and Drew pocketed his phone and shelved his memories of the last time he'd been out of a car on this stretch of the road so his senses could be on full alert.

BOOKS IN THE CARTER'S COVE ROMANCE SERIES

The Heartwood Sea (Book 1): She owns The Heartwood Inn. He needs the land the inn sits on to impress his boss. Neither one of them will give an inch. But will they give each other their hearts?

The Heartwood Inn (Book 2): She's excited to have a neighbor across the hall. He's got secrets he can never tell her. Will Olympia find a way to leave her past where it belongs so she can have a future with Chet?

The Heartwood Beach (Book 3): She's got a stalker. He's got a loud bark. Can Sheryl tame her bodyguard into a boyfriend?

The Heartwood Wedding (Book 4): He needs a reason not to go out with a journalist. She'd like a guaranteed date for the summer. They don't get along, so keeping Brad in the not-her-real-fiancé category should be easy for Celeste. Totally easy.

The Heartwood Chef (Book 5): They've been out before, and now they work in the same kitchen at The Heartwood Inn. Gwen isn't interested in getting anything filleted but fish, because Teagan's broken her heart before... Can Teagan and Gwen manage their professional relationship without letting feelings get in the way?

BOOKS IN THE HAWTHORNE HARBOR ROMANCE SERIES

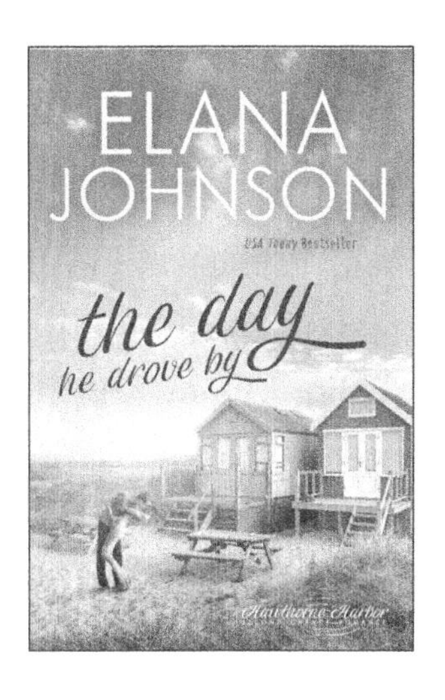

The Day He Drove By (Hawthorne Harbor Second Chance Romance, Book 1): A widowed florist, her ten-year-old daughter, and the paramedic who delivered the girl a decade earlier...

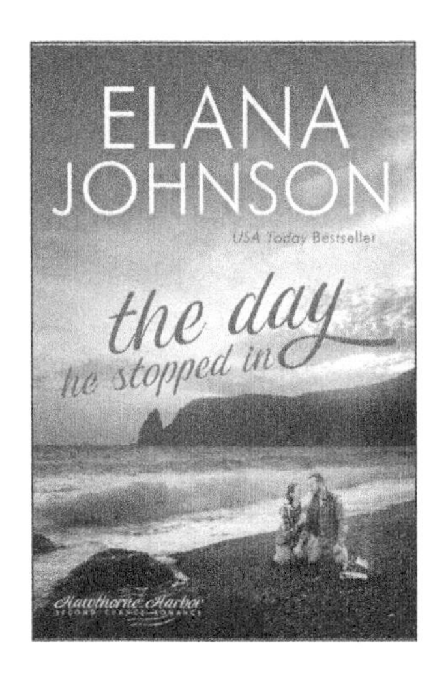

The Day He Stopped In (Hawthorne Harbor Second Chance Romance, Book 2): Janey Germaine is tired of entertaining tourists in Olympic National Park all day and trying to keep her twelve-year-old son occupied at night. When longtime friend and the Chief of Police, Adam Herrin, offers to take the boy on a ride-along one fall evening, Janey starts to see him in a different light. Do they have the courage to take their relationship out of the friend zone?

The Day He Said Hello (Hawthorne Harbor Second Chance Romance, Book 3): Bennett Patterson is content with his boring firefighting job and his big great dane...until he comes face-toface with his high school girlfriend, Jennie Zimmerman, who swore she'd never return to Hawthorne Harbor. Can they rekindle their old flame? Or will their opposite personalities keep them apart?

The Day He Let Go (Hawthorne Harbor Second Chance Romance, Book 4): Trent Baker is ready for another relationship, and he's hopeful he can find someone who wants him and to be a mother to his son. Lauren Michaels runs her own general contract company, and she's never thought she has a maternal bone in her body. But when she gets a second chance with the handsome K9 cop who blew her off when she first came to town, she can't say no... Can Trent and Lauren make their differences into strengths and build a family?

The Day He Came Home (Hawthorne Harbor Second Chance Romance, Book 5): A wounded Marine returns to Hawthorne Harbor years after the woman he was married to for exactly one week before she got an annulment...and then a baby nine months later. Can Hunter and Alice make a family out of past heartache?

The Day He Asked Again (Hawthorne Harbor Second Chance Romance, Book 6): A Coast Guard captain would rather spend his time on the sea...unless he's with the woman he's been crushing on for months. Can Brooklynn and Dave make their second chance stick?

BOOKS IN THE HOPE ETERNAL RANCH ROMANCE SERIES

Hopeful Cowboy, Book 1: Can Ginger and Nate find their happily-ever-after, keep up their duties on the ranch, and build a family? Or will the risk be too great for them both?

Overprotective Cowboy, Book 2: Can Ted and Emma face their pasts so they can truly be ready to step into the future together? Or will everything between them fall apart once the truth comes out?

Rugged Cowboy, Book 3: He's a cowboy mechanic with two kids and an ex-wife on the run. She connects better to horses than humans. Can Dallas and Jess find their way to each other at Hope Eternal Ranch?

Christmas Cowboy, Book 4: He needs to start a new story for his life. She's dealing with a lot of family issues. This Christmas, can Slate and Jill find solace in each other at Hope Eternal Ranch?

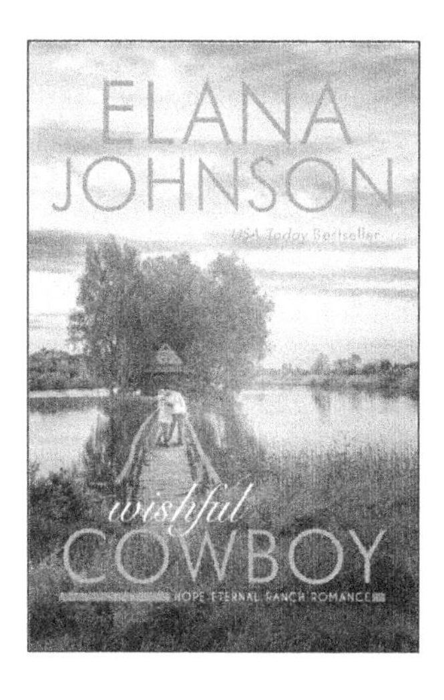

Wishful Cowboy, Book 5: He needs a place where he can thrive without his past haunting him. She's been waiting for the cowboy to return so she can confess her feelings. Can Luke and Hannah make their second chance into a forever love?

BOOKS IN THE GETAWAY BAY BILLIONAIRE ROMANCE SERIES

The Billionaire's Enemy (Book 1): A local island B&B owner hates the swanky high-rise hotel down the beach...but not the billionaire who owns it. Can she deal with strange summer weather, tourists, and falling in love?

The Billionaire's Driver (Book 2): A car service owner who's been driving the billionaire pineapple plantation owner for years finally gives him a birthday gift that opens his eyes to see her, the woman who's literally been right in front of him all this time. Can he open his heart to the possibility of true love?

The Billionaire's Fake Engagement (Book 3): A former poker player turned beach bum billionaire needs a date to a hospital gala, so he asks the beach yoga instructor his dog can't seem to stay away from. At the event, they get "engaged" to deter her former boyfriend from pursuing her. Can he move his fake fiancée into a real relationship?

The Billionaire's Cinderella (Book 4): The owner of a beach-side drink stand has taken more bad advice from rich men than humanly possible, which requires her to take a second job cleaning the home of a billionaire and global diamond mine owner. Can she put aside her preconceptions about rich men and make a relationship with him work?

The Billionaire's Bodyguard (Book 5): Women can be rich too...and this female billionaire can usually take care of herself just fine, thank you very much. But she has no defense against her past...or the gorgeous man she hires to protect her from it. He's her bodyguard, not her boyfriend. Will she be able to keep those two B-words separate or will she take her second chance to get her tropical happily-ever-after?

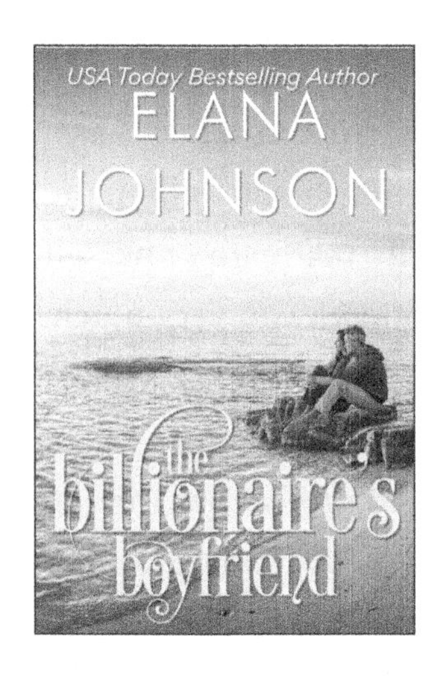

The Billionaire's Boyfriend (Book 6): Can a closet organizer fit herself into a single father's hectic life? Or will this female billionaire choose work over love...again?

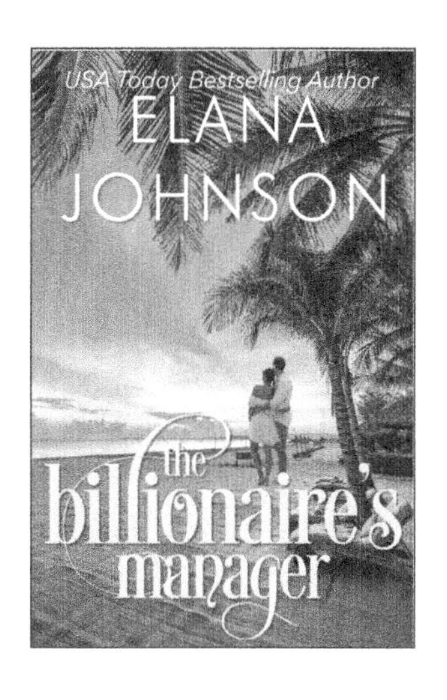

The Billionaire's Manager (Book 7): A billionaire who has a love affair with his job, his new bank manager, and how they bravely navigate the island of Getaway Bay...and their own ideas about each other.

The Billionaire's Ex-Wife (Book 8): A silver fox, a dating app, and the mistaken identity that brings this billionaire faceto-face with his ex-wife...

BOOKS IN THE BRIDES & BEACHES ROMANCE SERIES

The Island House (Book 1): Charlotte Madsen's whole world came crashing down six months ago with the words, "I met someone else." Her marriage of eleven years dissolved, and she left one island on the east coast for the island of Getaway Bay. She was not expecting a tall, handsome man to be flat on his back under the kitchen sink when she arrives at the supposedly abandoned house. But former Air Force pilot, Dawson Dane, has a charming devil-may-care personality, and Charlotte could use some happiness in her life.

Can Charlotte navigate the healing process to find love again?

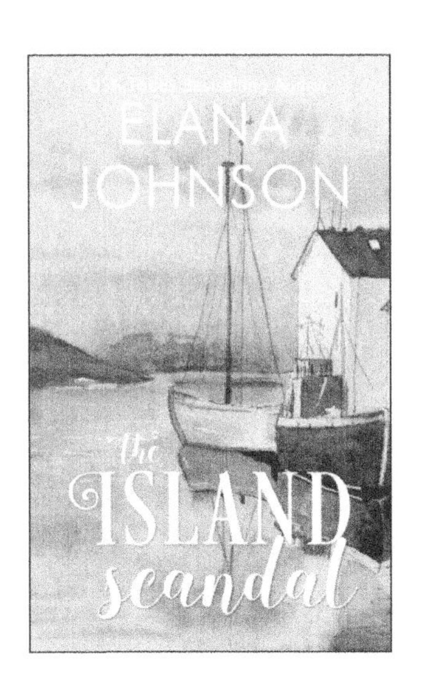

The Island Scandal (Book 2): Ashley Fox has known three things since age twelve: she was an excellent seamstress, what her wedding would look like, and that she'd never leave the island of Getaway Bay. Now, at age 35, he's been right about two of them, at least.

The Island Hideaway (Book 3): She's 37, single (except for the cat), and a synchronized swimmer looking to make some extra cash. Pathetic, right? She thinks so, and she's going to spend this summer housesitting a cliffside hideaway and coming up with a plan to turn her life around.

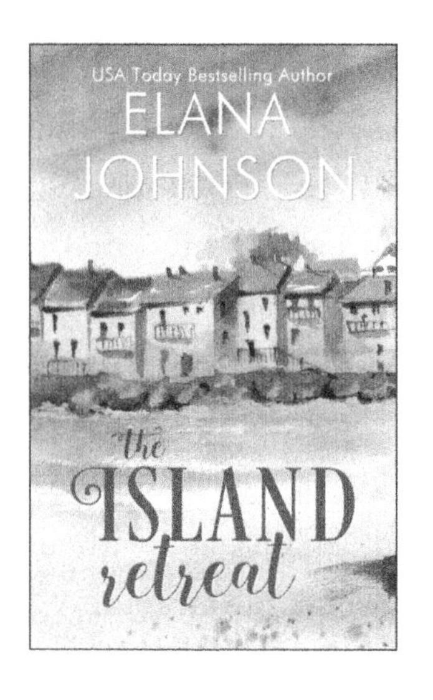

The Island Retreat (Book 4): Shannon's 35, divorced, and the highlight of her day is getting to the coffee shop before the morning rush. She tells herself that's fine, because she's got two cats and a past filled with emotional abuse. But she might be ready to heal so she can retreat into the arms of a man she's known for years...

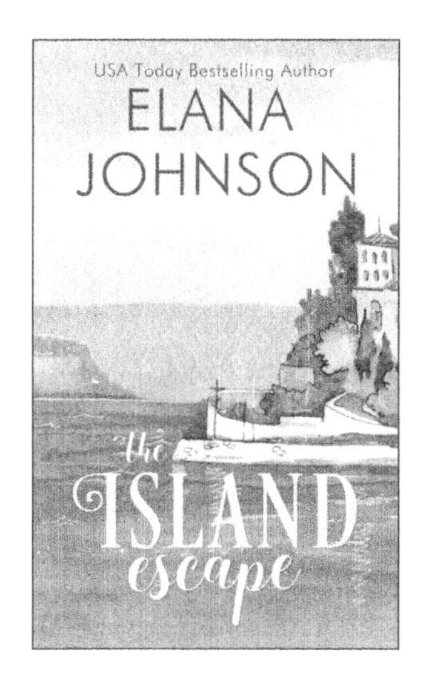

The Island Escape (Book 5): Riley Randall has spent eight years smiling at new brides, being excited for her friends as they find Mr. Right, and dating by a strict set of rules that she never breaks. But she might have to consider bending those rules ever so slightly if she wants an escape from the island...

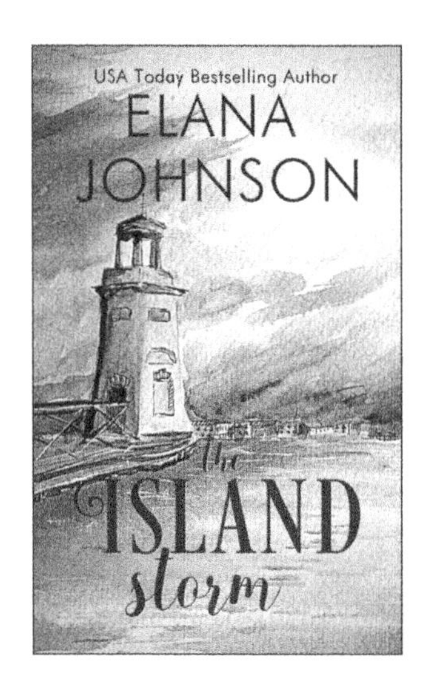

The Island Storm (Book 6): Lisa is 36, tired of the dating scene in Getaway Bay, and practically the only wedding planner at her company that hasn't found her own happy-ever-after. She's tried dating apps and blind dates...but could the company party put a man she's known for years into the spotlight?

The Island Wedding (Book 7): Deirdre is almost 40, estranged from her teenaged daughter, and determined not to feel sorry for herself. She does the best she can with the cards life has dealt her and she's dreaming of another island wedding...but it certainly can't happen with the widowed Chief of Police.

BOOKS IN THE STRANDED IN GETAWAY BAY ROMANCE SERIES

Love and Landslides (Book 1): A freak storm has her sliding down the mountain...right into the arms of her ex. As Eden and Holden spend time out in the wilds of Hawaii trying to survive, their old flame is rekindled. But with secrets and old feelings in the way, will Holden be able to take all the broken pieces of his life and put them back together in a way that makes sense? Or will he lose his heart and the reputation of his company because of a single landslide?

Kisses and Killer Whales (Book 2): Friends who ditch her. A pod of killer whales. A limping cruise ship. All reasons Iris finds herself stranded on an deserted island with the handsome Navy SEAL...

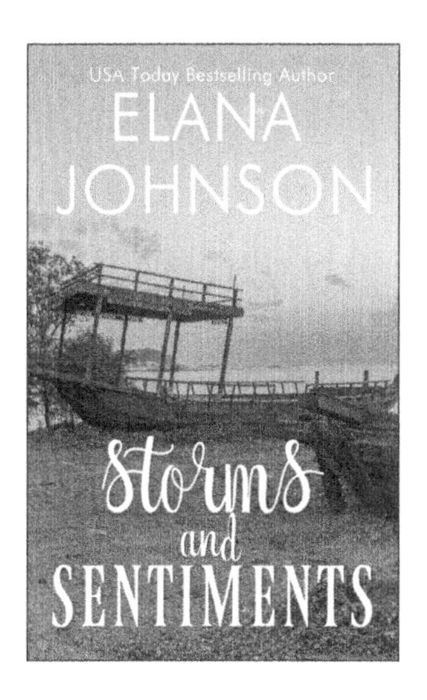

Storms and Sentiments (Book 3): He can throw a precision pass, but he's dead in the water in matters of the heart...

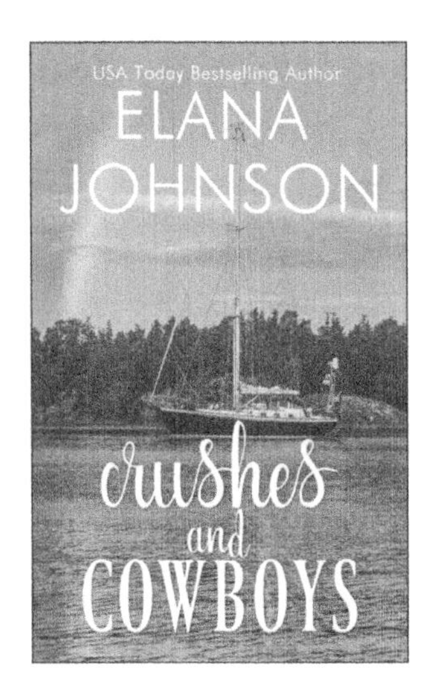

Crushes and Cowboys (Book 4): Tired of the dating scene, a cowboy billionaire puts up an Internet ad to find a woman to come out to a deserted island with him to see if they can make a love connection...

ABOUT ELANA

Elana Johnson is the USA Today bestselling author of dozens of clean and wholesome contemporary romance novels. She lives in Utah, where she mothers two fur babies, taxis her daughter to theater several times a week, and eats a lot of Ferrero Rocher while writing. Find her on her website at elanajohnson.com.

Made in the USA
Coppell, TX
27 October 2020